Mrs Rochester's Attic

Mrs Rochester's Attic

Tales of Madness, Strange Love and Deep, Dark Secrets.

Edited by Matthew Pegg

First published in the UK in 2017 by Mantle Lane Press

This collection is a work of fiction. Any reference to historical events, real
people or real locales are used fictitiously. Other names, characters, places and
incidents are products of the author's imagination, and any resemblance to
actual events or locales or persons, living or dead, is entirely coincidental.

ISBN 978-0-9932648-3-2

Mantle Lane Press
Mantle Arts
Springboard Centre
Mantle Lane
Coalville
LE67 3DW
www.mantlelanepress.co.uk
www.red-lighthouse.org.uk

Cover image by Jessamy Hawke
www.jessamyhawke.co.uk

Contents

Preface

The stories in this book explore madness, doomed relationships and secrets, inspired by the sad fate of the first Mrs Rochester in Charlotte Brontë's *Jane Eyre*. Hidden away by her husband, Mrs Rochester haunts the corridors of Thornfield Hall, and eventually burns it down, killing herself and blinding her husband.

The authors were not required to write directly about Mrs Rochester, Jane Eyre or the Brontës, but the stories had to contain a deep, dark secret, insanity or ill-fared love.
And what a wild mix they came up with. Some of the stories in this book are fantastical and some are realistic. Some are set in the past and others are contemporary. There's a wide mix of genres. But they all have a hint of the gothic and a tinge of strangeness.

Just the thing to read while hidden away in your own attic...

Introduction

The Real Mrs Rochester
Matthew Pegg

The importance of little known Brontë sister Dora has only become apparent in the past few years. Indeed her very existence has been hotly contested by literary critics hidebound by the restrictions of academe, such as the spurious need for such vague concepts as 'evidence'.

However it has been perfectly obvious to most uninformed yet right thinking people, that Patrick Brontë named his children in alphabetical order and therefore Anne, Branwell, Charlotte and Emily *must* have had a sibling who's name began with D and that the total lack of any evidence at all for such an overlooked Brontë sister (or brother) not to mention her (or his) contemporary impact on the literary world was no reason for not believing it to be true, and, as one opposing critic put it 'making up a lot of s**t'.

For many years these opposing views were entrenched, and indeed the general public were largely unaware of the raging controversy, or if they were aware, didn't give a flying fig. Even the Brontë Museum at Haworth completely ignored the potential existence of an extra Brontë or two in favour of concentrating on the less controversial existence of the more famous siblings, Anne, Charlotte, Emily and Wednesday.

However recent discoveries have confirmed that Dora Brontë did indeed exist, no really, and was in all probability the real life inspiration for mad Mrs Rochester in her sister Charlotte's seminal novel *Jane Eyre.* In June 2016 a battered wooden box full of hand written papers, bearing the inscription 'D. Brontë (Miss)', appeared on a well known online auction site. It was claimed that the box had been discovered in 2012 under the floorboards of the attic of Haworth Parsonage during renovations and 'saved from being thrown away'* by an eagle-eyed busybody.

In 2014 the box appeared on an edition of Antiques Roadshow. Their expert's verdict was inconclusive, stating that, if genuine, the box and its contents would be 'practically priceless', while pointing out that some of the Dora Brontë papers it contained seem to have been written in biro and that Haworth parsonage doesn't have an attic.

Its later appearance on Eb… on a well known online auction site, promised solutions to the literary controversy that had been ignored for almost a hundred years by everyone who had something better to do. Mantle Lane Press was determined to obtain the papers and prepared to petition the government for funds to ensure that this precious rarity remained in the country. In the event this was not necessary as the only other person bidding on the box was a bloke called Clive from Swindon. The auction was won and we paid all of £8.56, plus postage and packing for the a relic that would rock the literary establishment to its foundations.

The evidence contained in the box is compelling, if you're the kind of person likely to be compelled by this kind of thing. It reveals that as a teenager Dora Brontë was confined to the attic at Howarth and remained a virtual prisoner in her own home, outliving both Anne and Emily. Why this should have occurred is unclear. There are references in the papers to various peculiar

* a delicate euphemism for 'half-inched while nobody was looking'.

ailments she may have suffered from, mainly in the form of receipts from druggists. Maladies mentioned include, 'Yorkshire Ladies Hysteria', 'Congestion of the Nethers' and 'Mad as a Bag of Spanners' but it is unclear which of them might have led to her family mewing her up and forever denying her existence in such a cruel way.

The box contains diary entries, notes and lists, receipts for such items as 'Gilbert's Potent Blue Nitrogen Tonic' and 'Lady Ponsett's Finest Corset Crowbar' (pat pending). But of most interest to the literarily credulous are Dora Brontë's fictional writings. The box contains a few complete short stories, fragments of others, and scribbled ideas. There is also the first two and a half chapters of a novel *Griddlespike Hall* signed on the title page 'Dickinson Bell'. This suggests that Dora intended to join her sisters in publishing under a pseudonym, utilising the 'Bell' surname combined with a gender neutral forename, as they did. In the event this did not occur. In a diary entry Dora gives some clues to why this may have been, (although many of her entries have been redacted by another hand, possibly Charlotte's, making it hard to understand what she's blathering on about.)

> 'Charlotte complained that Griddlespike Hall was wholly unwholesome, a view with which I can not agree. In particular she pointed to the fate of Wyndham Griddlespike as being not suitable for anyone human to read, ever, especially the moment when the fox grabbed XXXXXXXXXX and XXXX his XXXXX and then the soldiers XXXX twice and then XXXXX XXX with his XXXXX. And this scene the very height of my creative endeavours! Has she not seen such things being done on the farm and

hardly winced at all? She also felt there were too many dolly-mops, flop-nobbies and pug-handlers in the scenes in London, though I do not believe she truly knows what they are.

Emily stated that she thought the whole thing was a bunch of XXX XXX XXXX. Dear Emily, always so honest, plain speaking and foul mouthed, that I must love her for it and can almost put aside the foaming delirium with which her words infused my brain, so that I must needs lie under the bed for three days straight, eating nothing but hard biscuit and drinking rainwater from the guttering through a straw.'

It also seems that as a child, Dora like her siblings wrote stories of imaginary worlds, that foreshadowed their work as adults. The box contained some of this juvenilia: pages written in tiny script and set in an island kingdom called Frottage, populated by African tribes people, British soldiers, French onion sellers, Scottish missionaries, and ruled over by Sir Robert Peel, a well known political figure of the day, inventor of the modern police force and the 'Copper's Little Helper'.

Confident that the box and its contents were genuine we still took the precaution of consulting experts at Leicester University and New Walk Museum, conscious of the opprobrium that would follow too credulous a response to what might be a clever literary hoax, of the same ilk as *The Secret Diaries of Adolf Hitler aged 53¾* and *The Julius Caesar Letters: Roman in the Gloamin'*.

The experts pointed out that there are certain anachronistic details in the stories, which include references to paper clips, female suffrage, bottled water and conceptual art. Rather than admit the deeply dodgy nature of our unexpectedly cheap auction find, we instead posited that Dora Brontë was writing science fiction or 'sci fi'. This means that she was one of the earliest proponents of 'sci-fi', writing speculatively about the future only a few decades after Mary Shelley published *Frankenstein* and its sequels *Bride of Frankenstein, Son of Frankenstein* and *Abbot and Costello meet Frankenstein.*

Thus reassured, we decided to publish a lavish edition of, *The Complete Works of Dora Brontë*, with a foreword by a photogenic academic, plus learned footnotes, a bibliography a nice red leather cover, and everything! This will take some time to cobble together, so in the meantime we decided to send all the snippets of Dora's stories and her notes that were found in the box to writers across the world and let them work them up, and, in effect, recreate for a modern audience the stories that Dora Brontë, the real Mrs Rochester, wrote, all alone in her attic, under lock and key, forgotten by the world.
And that dear reader is the book that you now hold in your hands.

[As a result of a court order we have been required to point out that some, or many, OK, *all* of the writers represented in this book strongly contest the suggestion made above that their work included herein is not entirely their own creation; and further state that they have never been sent any details, notes or fragments of any story or stories allegedly by Dora Brontë, or indeed any Brontë at all, past or present; and that everything in this introduction is wholly untrue and made up by us in a desperate effort to sell copies of this book.]

Like you'd believe that…

A Hint of Stardust
Anna Salonen

When I was a girl, I thought Blackwater Manor the finest house ever built. Every year my mother bundled me in travel rugs and handed me over to Uncle Alaric for the summer, and we boarded his extravagant airship, the first one built on Opal, for the half-day journey to Blackwater. I remember the cinnamon-scented wind in my hair, the grainy, gilded railing, warm from the late afternoon sun, and Aunt Vertiline's gowns billowing like gossamer cut-outs of sunset sky as she chased me around the deck while Uncle Alaric chortled and tried to keep us from knocking the teapot on his Sunday paper. But that was twenty years ago, when the stardust mines still made a profit. Before the war. Before Uncle Alaric shot himself.

I clutch my shawl and hold the brim of my hat tight against the wind. The old airship crackles and groans as the pilot manoeuvres it to the dock. The gilt has crumbled off the railings and mildew dots the faded rubber-coated fabric, barely visible under the dusting of snow. I finger my shabby, much-mended shawl, feel the rough patches through the thin wool of my gloves. Time has not been kind to either of us.

The cabin boy hops onto the dock, sending snow flying, and secures the craft. When he is finished he offers me his hand.

'Careful, Miss. It's slippery.'

I nod and thank the sky-gods I wore my riding boots. Not that I have any silk slippers left. Even the boots are hand-me-downs, my friend Victoria's rejects.

'Would you like me to accompany you, Miss Devitt?' the pilot asks, casting a longing look at the warm cabin behind us.

'No, I shall manage.' I'd rather face my ghosts alone, anyhow.

I leave the men to their hot tea and pipe tobacco and head for the house. The snow is kind; it covers the ravages of time and, just for a moment, lets me pretend I'm coming home from yet another hunting party, the rowdy young men competing over the privilege of drinking hot chocolate at my feet. I pass the familiar pine tree, shipped from Terra at great expense. That's where Berard first proposed to me, where I turned him down. I can almost see him, playing with the motherless dusklynx cub in the snow. They had to shoot it after a few months when it mauled one of the footmen, and Uncle Alaric mounted it standing on its hind legs and placed a silver bowl in its paws for calling cards. He always had a strange sense of humour.

As I get closer to the house, the illusion shatters. Broken windows squint down at me, and shutters snap and rattle in the wind. I can't face going inside yet, so I go around and admire the Blackwater Falls, frozen into obsidian pillars over the quarry pits. The hanging gardens, once Aunt Vertiline's pride and joy, are only dead tangles now, and the shattered sculptures just strange shapes under the snow.

A gust of wind blows snow in my face. I lick a few stray flakes from my lips. Smoke and the cinnamon hint of stardust, just like the icicles we used to snap off the potting shed walls as children. Berard liked to put them in his sourberry tonics when we were older. This is where I refused him the second time. He didn't ask me again after that. I haven't seen him in ten years. Where is he now? Probably married to some plump beauty, doting over half-a-dozen fat-cheeked children.

I turn away. It's too cold to stand here reminiscing. Besides, the men have probably finished their tea by now and will come after me if I don't return soon. I have to get this done. The buyers will take possession tomorrow, and I should check for valuables. Maybe a family heirloom or two eluded the auctioneer's sharp eye? I owe it to Uncle Alaric to make certain.

The door hangs off its hinges, but after a good shove it shifts enough that I can duck inside. I jiggle the light-beads on my wrist and they flicker to life. Stardust is strange like that. Uncle Alaric gave the beads to me when I was nine. They're the only thing I refuse to sell.

I walk through the foyer and step into Uncle Alaric's study. A flash of teeth and glittering eyes in the darkness; an animal, ready to pounce. I scream and I'm almost out the door when I notice the flash of silver and my scream turns into a strangled laugh. The shadowlynx. Its cracked teeth gleam yellow and most of the hair has fallen out, leaving bald patches all over, but the damned thing is still clutching the silver bowl with the unwavering determination of the dead. I try to tug the bowl away, but it's stuck. Maybe one of the men can get it later.

Uncle Alaric's portrait is still on the wall. It's faded and blue with mould, but his eyes seem to follow me as I search the room. Nothing worth taking, just some crumbling papers and books that stink of rot. Then I notice something behind the fallen lynx. A silver frame, almost black. I wipe the moisture off the glass. Berard, in his airship captain's uniform, moustache impeccably trimmed. It's the first picture he sent me, a token of an old man's fragile ego. When I met him he wasn't the steely-eyed thirty-year-old in the photo, but a balding gentleman in his late fifties, ancient to a girl of sixteen.

I slip the photograph in my valise and move on. There's

nothing more on the ground floor except for rusty pots and pans in the kitchen, so I ascend the obsidian staircase to the ballroom. Water damage discolours the ceiling, and snowflakes drift from where the roof has fallen in. The oak panels, another extravagance, are warped and cracked, but I can still make out the mural on the wall. Such a silly thing, classical ruins and columns set in Opal's alien landscape. The Blackwater Falls are well done, though.

I sit in a ruined chair and watch the snow fall. It's hard to believe this is where we danced with ambassadors and kings and drank champagne flecked with stardust in our expensive gowns. We were like butterflies in the field, oblivious to the death and decay to come. I catch a glimpse of myself in the blackened mirror, my drab mourning suit, grey shawl, and gloves. I've gone from butterfly to moth.

The stairs creak, and I turn. I expect to see one of the men from the ship, but it's someone else. It takes me a moment to recognize him, but the neat moustache and military bearing give him away. It's Berard.

'What are you doing here?' I blurt out.

'I saw the footprints and decided to investigate. I come to walk in the garden sometimes.'

'Oh.' Berard always liked the gardens in winter, the strange, exotic plants sleeping under the snow. I only saw dead things, even back then.

He looks around, rubs his bottom lip where his pipe usually rests. 'I hate to see the old place like this, gone to ruin.'

I turn away, pull my shawl tighter. I don't want him to look at me, to see the moth. I want him to remember the butterfly.

Berard doesn't seem to notice. He touches my arm, feather-light like the brush of a snowy owl's wing. 'We could make it great again.'

I stare at him, uncomprehending. Could he still care? The look in his eye tells me he does. I stop to consider. He's offering me an easy life. Comfort. Companionship. The old days back. Maybe Blackwater Manor is only sleeping under the snow? I want to say yes and bring Blackwater to life like the Spring Maiden in Aunt Vertiline's fairy stories, but in my heart I know I can't. I didn't love Berard then and I don't now. Besides, I'm too old to play with fire. The life of a moth isn't so arduous. The name of Devitt still carries some weight in society; I'll always have a place to sleep, the ambition of social climbers guarantees that. It will have to do.

Gently I remove his hand from my shoulder and kiss his cold, smooth cheek.

A wan smile breaks through his frown.

'Goodbye, my sweet Ada.'

'Goodbye, Berard.'

I leave him in the ballroom. Snowflakes settle on his stiff shoulders, set against the cold. I feel him at the window as I make my way back to the dock, but I don't look back.

The airship pilot is waiting for me.

'Ready to leave, Miss?'

'Yes.'

The old manor grows farther away. The moon rises, the snow sparkles silver, like stardust. Only one set of footprints mars the snow. Soon they, too, will be gone, swept away by the winter winds.

A Warning to Young Ladies
Jill Hand

Imprisonment in a cramped and dusty room at the top of a gloomy, isolated mansion is not a state conducive to peace of mind. That is a fact of which I am quite confident, having experienced it for myself.

It is a wonder I didn't go mad.

My name is Bertha Antoinetta Mason, former captive of Thornfield Hall in the cold and miserable place that is Yorkshire, England. Before I came to Thornfield Hall I lived in paradise, or rather in Jamaica, which is a close approximation of that other, lost paradise. Jamaica was everything Yorkshire is not: hot and lush, mountainous and untamed. The streets of Kingston, where I lived as a child, were lined with towering palm trees. If the fancy took me, I could lean out of my bedroom window and pick bananas, which our cook would fry and serve with red snapper. Everywhere were deliciously scented flowers - jasmine, angel's trumpet, bougainville - spilling from wrought-iron planters suspended from the lampposts and twining up the fronts of houses. It was a feast for the nose as well as for the eyes.

But then my father died, and my grieving mother took me away to Montchanin, her plantation in Montego Bay, the ownership of which came to her from her late father. I was lonely, bored and miserable. My mother, who was a Creole of mixed

French and English blood, no longer exhibited her former typically French gaiety and love of entertaining but became a recluse, shutting herself up in her bedchamber, where she made a sort of shrine out of my father's gloves, hairbrushes and shaving scuttle, which she arranged on a crepe-draped mahogany table. She spent most of her time in there, weeping and talking to my father's portrait.

My brother Richard having departed for England, the running of the plantation was left to the overseer, a ne'er-do-well Irishman who preferred to drink rum rather than see to it that the negroes did their work properly.

Slavery had been abolished in the West Indies not long before and the negroes drank rum in celebration of having become free men and women. They made only a desultory attempt to cultivate and harvest the sugarcane that was the plantation's main crop. The island's economy was in shambles and many of the negroes had become insolent and openly contemptuous of their former masters. White people slept with pistols under their pillows in dread of a revolution like the one that swept Haiti at the end of the last century.

The oppressive heat was unrelieved the summer I turned twenty. Wildfires burned out of control in the mountains and there was a palpable sense of danger everywhere. Montchanin no longer felt safe but where else was I to go? I had no husband, and my money was tied up in land that no-one wanted to buy because they feared being hacked to death by machete-wielding practitioners of the local sorcery called obeah. I was trapped.

Then one day, just as in that Biblical paradise, a snake appeared and tempted me, as the snake who was Satan tempted Eve.

This particular snake was six feet high, stern-featured, heavy-browed, shaggy-haired and was called Edward Fairfax Rochester.

I did not know it at the time but he was a brute, a liar, a thief, and a philanderer. He was also that exalted creature known as an English gentleman, before whom three-quarters of the globe's inhabitants prostrate themselves in adoration.

I entered the parlour one day, having returned from a ride, to find my mother seated with a man. They both held little glasses of sherry and the man was smoking a black cheroot. I gaped in astonishment. My mother had never permitted my father or my brother to smoke in the house.

'Here is Bertha now,' my mother said.

The man rose to his feet, exhaled a cloud of foul-smelling smoke, and looked me over, grinning.

'Hello, Miss Mason. I am very pleased to make your acquaintance. Your brother told me all about you. I must say that his effusive description did you justice,' he said, bowing.

He said he had met my brother in London and Richard bade him to go to Jamaica and make the acquaintance of my mother. He did not disclose where he had encountered Richard, but looking back, I now suspect that it was probably over a gaming table, or in one of the great metropolis's less savoury resorts.

Mr Rochester stayed with us for three days. On the second day, during a stroll in which I pointed out the plantation's fields (rapidly becoming weed-choked) the cattle (lean and unhappy-looking) and the outbuildings (in need of a fresh coat of paint) he asked for the privilege of being called Edward. In return he announced that he would call me Bertha. On the third day he confessed that he had fallen in love with me.

The prospect of having a man as tall and masterful as Edward Rochester in love with me was a pleasurable one. Silly girl that I was, I had read novels in which the heroine was told by some dark-browed, commanding gentleman that he loved her so I knew exactly how to respond.

'Good heavens, sir. I hardly know what to say,' I told him, modestly lowering my eyes. I saw a little green lizard about to run beneath my skirts. I brushed it away with the toe of my shoe.

'Say you love me too,' Edward entreated, clasping my hands in his.

'All right,' I said, looking around for the lizard, which had scurried off somewhere. 'I love you too.'

'Good,' he said, giving his shaggy head a curt, businesslike nod. 'Your mother has given me permission to marry you. We leave for Kingston this afternoon. We shall be married there and then board a ship sailing for England first thing in the morning.'

'So soon? What about notifying my friends, and planning a wedding party, and…and everything else?' I said weakly. Events were moving too rapidly. I had always thought that a proposal of marriage was a thing to be savoured and gloated over. Especially delightful was the prospect of telling one's friends and acquaintances who weren't fortunate enough to be engaged.

Edward frowned and narrowed his eyes. It was the first time he glowered at me and I found myself trembling. For a moment I thought he would strike me, but them he smiled and lit a cheroot.

'I love you too much to wait even one more day for you to become my bride,' he said, shaking out the Lucifer and letting it fall to the ground. 'Besides, I've booked passage for two on a ship leaving to-morrow as soon as the tide goes out. Your mother gave her consent. You have nothing to keep you here. When we get to England I'll take you to the best dressmaker in London, and we'll go to routs and balls and be as happy as two turtledoves in a nest.'

I considered his proposition. 'This is your chance to escape. You'll be a married lady and have fine clothes and a carriage and a home of your own. Say yes,' whispered a greedy little voice in my head.

'Yes,' I said. 'That sounds lovely.'

'Then kiss me, and we shall seal our bliss,' said Edward, in dramatic tones that the actor Charles Kemble might have envied. He threw down his cheroot, stamped it out with his boot heel and took me in his arms.

That kiss was the first of many disappointments in my life with Edward. If you have never kissed a man who habitually smokes cheroots and has breakfasted on jerk-spiced goat stew then you are fortunate indeed. I felt my gorge rise as our lips locked.

He released me and I staggered back a couple of paces, fearing I might become ill. Edward beamed proudly, no doubt thinking me overcome by his kiss, which I was, but not in the way that he intended.

The next thing I knew we were married in a church vestry by a clergyman with no teeth. He mumbled so reading the wedding ceremony that he may well have been reciting a ship's cargo manifest. Then we were aboard a ship, which pitched and rolled its way to England so enthusiastically that I feared at any moment we might be capsized and drowned. Edward divided his time between being copiously seasick into a china bowl held by me, playing piquet and vingt-et-un with other gentlemen in the smoking saloon, and collapsing, quite intoxicated, on top of me in the narrow bunk in our cabin.

'You know what I'd like?' he said to me as he scrabbled beneath my petticoats.

'What?' I asked, dreading the answer.

'A baby. A lil' baby boy that looks jes' like me,' he slurred drunkenly. 'I'll teach 'im to ride, an' to shoot, an' play cards, an' be a gennel' man. Go to Eaton. Play cricket. Go out to Africa an' order the fuzzy-wuzzies aroun'.'

The prospect of another Edward Fairfax Rochester filled me with horror. Fortunately, Edward was usually too drunk to be able to complete the act that makes babies. Although I had seen animals coupling I had embraced the fond hope that it was done differently among human beings. That was not so. In fact, the bulls that I'd seen mounting cows seemed more tenderly solicitous of the cows than Edward was to me as he fumbled and thrust and cursed and breathed rank fumes of tobacco and liquor in my face.

When the sea was calm and the ship left off threatening to plunge us down to Davy Jones' Locker I used to walk on deck and take the air. It lifted my spirits to see the soaring gulls and schools of dolphins. I was returning from doing so one morning when I encountered Edward in the companionway outside our cabin.

'Where have you been?' he asked with a face like thunder.

I told him I'd been walking on deck.

'Anything else?'

'No,' I said, confused. 'Just walking.'

He seized me by the arm and pulled me roughly into our cabin, kicking the door shut behind us.

'Liar!' he roared. 'I saw you talking to a sailor. Ladies don't hang about talking to sailors. Who knows what else you've been up to while I have been otherwise occupied?' With that he raised his fist and struck me in the eye.

I felt ashamed. Not angry, as I would be now, but deeply ashamed. I had encountered a sailor, who was doing something with a rope. He bid me good-morning and I responded in kind. Apparently it had been wrong of me. I stayed in the cabin for the rest of the voyage, nursing my black eye - the first of many I was to receive from Edward - and resolving not to anger him again.

Upon arriving in London, Edward took me directly to Coutt's and Company, a bank in the Strand, where I learned to my surprise that my father had made arrangements for me to receive five hundred pounds upon my marriage and another two hundred every year. I was an heiress!

Edward presented me to an old man in a snuff-colored waistcoat who was seated behind a desk. He showed him our marriage certificate, and demanded the five hundred pounds, payable immediately.

'Certainly, sir! Right away. And may I offer my sincere felicitations upon your nuptials on behalf of Coutt's and…'

Edward cut him off. 'Give me the money,' he growled, holding out a valise like a highwayman who had ordered a coach's passengers to stand and deliver.

There was to be no visit to the finest dressmaker in London, as he had promised. I was weary from our journey and had hoped to acclimate myself to being on dry land again by taking in the sights of London. Instead, Edward hustled me into a coach bound for Yorkshire.

'Can't we stay at your house in Belgrave Square for a few days?' I begged him.

No, he replied. The house was let to tenants and the lease wouldn't be up for another six months. Perhaps then we could stay there.

That, of course, was a lie. Edward had lost the house in Belgrave Square in a game of cards. That was the reason he'd married me: for my money.

'Your fortune is not a great one, but at least it's something. I owe money to my tailor and my bootmaker and my gunsmith and the butcher, the baker, and the candlestick maker. I would rather not be thrown into debtor's prison,' he said sullenly, lighting another cheroot and flicking the spent Lucifer out the coach window. 'Miss Amelia Fitzgibbons has a thousand a year. I would have married her despite her crossed eyes and hunched back, but her father dislikes me.'

I didn't blame Mr Fitzgibbons; I disliked Edward too, but there was nothing to be done about it. We were married and I must make the best of it. And so we bounced and rattled our way to Thornfield Hall.

There is a cave in the American state of Kentucky that is famous for its vast, gloomy, high-ceilinged chambers that echo with emptiness. Thornfield Hall was like that cave. The air in its cavernous rooms always felt chilly, even at the height of summer. It was a forbidding and inhospitable house and in that regard it was perfectly suited to its owner.

Edward left after two weeks, claiming to have pressing matters to attend to in Paris. I was relieved to see him go. As I lay in bed with a sick headache, I could hear him conferring with the housekeeper, Mrs Fairfax, in the corridor outside my room. Mrs Fairfax seemed well-disposed toward me at first, but Edward put an end to that.

'See to it that she makes no calls, and receives no visitors. She needs rest, and quiet,' he told her.

'Is it because there is to be a blessed event? A dear little angel to come amongst us and brighten our days? O, how I will kiss its little toes!' she said fervently. Mrs Fairfax was a distant relation of Edward's and was able to take more liberties than most servants.

'Damned if I know,' replied Edward.

'Then why is she to make no calls, and receive none?' I could hear the floorboards creak as the housekeeper moved closer to hear her employer's reply.

Edward sighed heavily and I strained to hear. 'Because she is mad, quite, quite mad.'

'No!' breathed Mrs Fairfax, sounding equal parts horrified and delighted. There is nothing servants - even superior serv-ants - like better than scandal.

'I am afraid so. Bad blood runs in her family. Insanity going back three generations. Her mother is a drunkard and…breathe not a word of this to anyone, Alice, I implore you, but she is said to have negro ancestry.'

'Good gracious!' said Mrs Fairfax.

I could hear a scraping sound as Edward lit another of his cheroots. 'She's also part French. Creole they call it.'

Mrs Fairfax gave a little shriek. Apparently being French was worse than being a negress. 'O, the French are a wicked, villain-ous race! Why ever did you marry her, knowing all that?'

'Because I did not know it. Her brother tricked me into mar-rying her. He said she was rich, and as you can see, she is hand-some,' he said heavily.

'But French! And mad! I fear we shall all be murdered in our sleep,' moaned Mrs Fairfax.

Edward said there was no need to fear. I was placid most of the time, but any excitement, even so slight a one as a call from a lady or the vicar might cause me to fly into a frenzy. It was best not to allow me see anyone other than herself and the other female servants.

'I am ashamed to say it, but she had an assignation with a sailor on board the ship as we came over here,' he told her. I clenched my fists and ground my teeth when I heard that. What a lying scoundrel!

'Do not be perturbed. I'll see to it that she is kept quiet, and receives no callers,' promised Mrs Fairfax.

She accomplished that by dosing me with generous table-spoonfuls of thick, sticky liquid from a bottle labelled 'Mother

Dortle's Superior Soothing Syrup'. Mother Dortle was profligate in her approach to apothecary recipes in that the soothing syrup contained not only herbs and honey but also laudanum and a fair amount of alcohol. I was soothed into a state of insensibility for the next thirteen years.

Thirteen years sounds like a long time, but up in the attic where Edward eventually commanded that I be kept, time passed remarkably rapidly. I would wander drowsily to the window one day, a journey that seemed to take as long as a trek across the sands of Arabia but was in reality only a few yards, and look outside to see green buds beginning to appear on the trees. The next time I looked, the landscape would be blanketed in snow.

'It was spring a few days ago and now it is winter. How odd! The seasons pass remarkably swiftly here,' I said to my father, who was no longer dead. He had come back to life and had gone on a journey to India to bring me an elephant and a monkey, which were in the kitchen, doing tricks for the servants and the little girl whom Edward insisted was his ward, but whom I suspected was his own daughter. Father agreed that the climate in England was indeed remarkably changeable.

'Have a banana; there is a banana tree growing right over there,' he suggested, pointing.

The tree had rubbery, glossy green leaves and was growing out of the middle of a chaise longue with a splintered arm and worn velvet upholstery. I stretched out my hand to grasp a ripe yellow banana only to fall asleep. The attic was a sleepy kind of place. When I awakened hours - or days - later, Father was gone and my hand was still outstretched, reaching for a phantom banana.

I was rescued by a deck of cards.

It happened like this: one night as I wandered through the endless, drafty corridors of Thornfield Hall, as I did sometimes when my nurse cum jailer Grace Poole failed to lock the door to my attic room, I discovered a deck of cards on an inlaid table in the long gallery. Also on the table were an empty bottle of wine and a glass with the stub of a cheroot floating in a half-inch of red liquid at the bottom, indicating Edward had been there recently. I idly took up the cards and continued on my wandering, peeking in at the young woman whom Edward had hired as governess to his so-called ward, Adèle, daughter of a rope-dancer whom Edward had met in Paris. I had seen the governess, a sly little item named Jane, making cow's eyes at Edward one time as they walked in the grounds below my attic window. I wasn't the least bit disturbed. By the look of her simpering face that turned coldly calculating when she thought he wasn't looking, they richly deserved one another.

Silently closing the door of Jane's room, I walked on, turning a corner of the corridor and coming face to face with a hag! The hag's black hair was wild and tangled, with thick streaks of white at the temples. Her eyes were red and mad and her face was slack and the colour of dough. I drew back, horrified. The hag did the same. I leaned forward. The hag leaned forward also and peered at me in disbelief. The hag was me, reflected in a looking glass.

I wept then, and retreated to my attic room. Grace Poole snored in her armchair, oblivious to my absence and subsequent return. I looked at the bottle of soothing syrup and at the spoon lying beside it. I was reaching out to take it up when I realized I was still holding onto the deck of cards. If I was to ever leave this place alive I needed my wits about me. No more soothing syrup, instead I formulated a plan.

I shook Grace awake. 'Let us play cards,' I said.

Grace Poole was not pleased to be awakened, but she was cheered by the prospect of a few hands of cards, with my gold ear-rings as the prize, if she won.

'I have no holes in my earlobes. I can't wear 'em,' she protested, upon realizing they were for pierced ears.

'I will make some holes for you, with a sewing needle,' I told her.

'Will it hurt?' she asked.

'A little, but you can drink a glass of gin first, and it won't be so bad,' I replied.

That reassured her. 'All right. What'll we play?'

We played klaberjass, a game a Dutch friend of my father had taught him and he, in turn taught me. We played piquet and vingt-et-un. We played two-handed euchre. We played briscola. The cards distracted me from wanting the soothing syrup. My ear-rings went back and forth between Grace and me many times over the ensuing months. Grace had a knack for cards and was a formidable adversary. I grew proficient at remembering which cards had been drawn and which remained in the deck. When Grace wasn't there, I entertained myself by practising fancy shuffles and playing patience. The soothing syrup I poured out the window, and I feigned drowsiness when Mrs Fairfax came to check up on me.

One day she brought a letter and a parcel from my mother. Both had been opened.

'I am sorry to tell you that your mother is dead. Mr Rochester says she died of a cancer in the breast,' said Mrs Fairfax. She handed me the letter and the parcel, which contained an embroidered pillow, wrapped in one of my mother's old shawls, and left the room, locking the door behind her.

My poor mama! I withdrew the letter from its envelope and with trembling hands read what she had written.

'My darling Bertha,' it began. 'I will soon join your dear Papa. Do not weep for me, but instead recall the happy times when we were all together. You have my heart. Hold this pillow I have stitched for you tightly to your bosom if ever you are in need of a mother's love and assistance. My jewel, farewell!

Your Mama.'

I cried, thinking I would never see my mother again, not on this earth, at least. I wrapped the shawl around my shoulders, inhaling the familiar fragrance of my mother's perfume. Then I took up the letter again. I furrowed my brow. Mama had never called me her jewel. There was a funny slip of the pen at the end of the word, making it look almost like 'jewels,' plural.

My heart thumping with excitement, I prodded the pillow. There was something lumpy in the centre. My heart. My jewels. A few snips of a scissors revealed mama's heart-shaped diamond brooch, her pearls, and her ruby and emerald bracelets nestled in a bed of sawdust. I cried some more, out of relief as well as sorrow. Now I had a means of escaping Edward.

You may have heard about the fire that destroyed Thornfield Hall. Edward set it, in a rash attempt to collect the insurance he'd taken out on the drafty old place. Typically, he made a hash of things and burned himself while attempting to light whatever he poured onto the floorboards, with one of his Lucifers. He lost a hand, and an eye. Although it is not very Christian of me, I cannot say that I am sorry.

I am now known as Madame Montchanin, purported widow of a Jamaican planter, and a resident of Saint-Rémy-de-Provence. The fields around my villa are filled not with sugar cane but with lavender. The scent lifts my heart.

I still play cards. I give fashionable little soirées where I instruct the young ladies of the town in the finer points of piquet and vingt-et-un. Occasionally I give them advice. I warn them to watch out for men who profess to love them but who only love their gold. I tell them the story of a foolish girl I once knew who made an unhappy bargain with a snake and lived to regret it. I tell them to never allow themselves to be soothed and dulled and locked away in an attic, for they may not be fortunate enough to escape. Then I shuffle the cards, and deal.

Honey for the Bag Lady
Valentine Williams

Her bag wasn't in its usual place, Sarah noticed. It was a large, well-made leather bag containing a quantity of pockets and zipped compartments. and the cat was sitting on top of it, pretending to be asleep, but Sarah could see one yellow eye squinting at her, half open.

'Off!' she cried, furious, pulling the long black strap away from the chair. The cat pretended it had been about to move anyway and descended from the chair with dignity. The bag was covered in cat hair. Sarah grabbed it and rummaged in the outside pockets for her travel pass. No luck. The cat gave her an insolent look and sauntered to the door. Where was her travel pass? Might it have dropped inside the bag?

Sarah thrust her hand deep into the bag and was startled that her hand went in right up to the elbow. And there was still no sign of the pass. Her fingers touched something else; something she did not recognise. It felt greasy and brittle. A piece broke off in her hand and she pulled it out. There was a smell of beeswax and honey.

'Rob, can you come here a moment?'

'Problem?' He wasn't really interested; Sarah was always losing things or wanting something fixing.

'Look. I just pulled this out of my handbag.' She held out

the fragment of honeycomb. He looked at it suspiciously. It was sticky.

'Out of your bag? How on earth could it have got in there?'

Sarah's eyebrows went up.

'I don't know. I put my hand into my bag to find my bus pass, and then I pulled this out. There's more of it in there. Can you look inside it for me?'

He put his ear to the bag. There was a quiet humming in the depths. The cat was watching them from the cat flap, ready to exit quickly.

'You must have left it somewhere outside, for a bee to get in. I'll empty it in the garden, so whatever's in there can fly away.'

'Thanks.'

He took the bag gingerly, holding it closed. It wasn't large enough to contain a whole honeycomb, surely? It was, he reckoned, about twenty five centimetres in depth. She was lucky whatever was in the bag hadn't stung her. He held it upside down over the concrete flags of the patio and shook it. The cat watched from a safe distance, sceptically. But nothing came out. He shook it again. Nothing happened. Still he could hear faint buzzing. He tried to open the neck of the bag a little wider so he could see inside. Pinpricks of light flashed in the depths of the bag. The humming ceased. He nearly put his hand in, then changed his mind.

'Got a torch?' he shouted. 'Bring me that torch that's under the sink, can you?'

'What have you found? Anything?'

'Nothing came out when I shook it.'

'Have you put your hand inside?'

'No. And I'm not going to.' If this was some horrible joke or trick he'd be really angry. Sarah found the torch. He held the bag open while she shone the torch inside. Tiny pin pricks of light moved around in the darkness.

'There's something in there moving.'

'What is it? Can you see?' The tiny lights retreated to the bottom of the bag and slowly went out. Then the bag gave a slight squirm in his hands and he almost dropped it.

'I'm going to take the bag and dump it in the deep freeze. That should sort it out. Show me that piece you pulled out, the one you showed me.'

But Sarah couldn't find it. She'd put it on the table, she was sure she had. Maybe the cat, who had come indoors again, had knocked it off.

'I don't know what happened to it.'

'Oh for heavens' sake, Sarah.' He fetched a bamboo cane from the flowerbed and pushed it into the bag. He stopped when the cane kept on going and his hand became dangerously close to the opening. 'This is crazy. Your bag isn't that deep.'

'I know.'

The neck of the bag twitched. A bee squeezed through the gap and flew off, followed by another bee, and another. A stream of bees flew off towards the garden. The cats' eyes moved sideways and back, following them. The bees vanished in the next garden.

'I'm glad they left,' said Sarah. 'I hope the bag's not all sticky inside.' She still hadn't found her travel pass, or her reading glasses, or the letter she had meant to post to her aunt. She had her purse, this time, in her shopping bag, but that was all.

Rob took the bag, holding it carefully by the strap and took it to the garage. He opened the freezer and dropped the bag inside. Cold steam escaped from the freezer; he was grateful for it. Whatever was in the bag could turn to ice for all he cared.

He banged the lid down harder than he meant to. A faint noise came from inside the cabinet. He ignored it; it was most likely ice dislodged from the lid or something. If Sarah wasn't such a slattern it would have been defrosted properly and the contents properly labelled and stored, instead of them being dumped in the bottom in various bags and boxes. They'd bought the freezer from a friend whose shop was closing down. A sticky residue of ice-cream carton bases still lingered in the cold metallic corners. The bag, he imagined, would soon be stuck to the base as well.

Maybe he should get it out and have a look? Had he really seen tiny lights inside it?

The cat jumped up onto the lid and looked at him, questioningly. He pushed it off. Sarah found her travel pass in her jacket pocket and held it up to show him:

'You'll never guess where I found it! By the way, how long do you think I need to keep my bag in the freezer?'

'Overnight should do it. Where are you going?'

'Just round to see Celia. You'll be okay?

'I'll have to be,' he said grumpily 'You give me no choice.' Sarah sighed and gave him a false smile as she left. He felt suddenly bereft. In the living room he dozed off in front of the TV, then got up and made himself some supper, before realising that Sarah wasn't back. He thought about the black leather bag still in the freezer. Did he need to wait until morning to get it out? He unlocked the side door into the garage and went to the freezer. The cat jumped down from its perch on the window sill and followed him. He lifted the heavy white lid of the freezer slowly and peered inside. There wasn't a good light in the garage, but he could make out a dark stiff shape at the bottom, covered in ice crystals. The cat at his feet rubbed itself around his ankle. He pushed it away with his foot. He reached his arms in slowly and took hold of the bag; pulled it up and out of the freezer. The cat suddenly spat and gave a hiss and bolted for the open door to the house.

He handled the bag slowly, running his fingers along the zip.

Then he undid it. He could hear Sarah's key in the lock.

'Hello? I'm home.'

'So I see.'

'What are you doing with my bag?'

'Looking to see what all the fuss was about.'

'And? What have you found out? What about the bees?'

'Oh, the bees... Here, see for yourself.' She approached cautiously. 'Don't worry, they'll all be frozen solid. That is, if there are any.'

'What do you mean? You saw them!'

'No darling, you saw them. You found that piece of honeycomb that disappeared. Remember? You really think there were bees in your bag?'

Sarah suddenly began to cry. The cat looked sympathetically at her. Rob smiled and looked away. His foot crunched something sticky. Honeycomb.

What the Dollhouse Said
Karen Bovenmyer

The first time I see Eleanor, she gets on the bus in uneven pig-tails wearing a faded flower-print dress. 'Don't sit by me, new girl,' I think. 'Don't sit by me.' Billy pokes me in the back of the head with a pencil, tries to make me cry, but he sees her quick and stops. I know he's watching her. Coyote boys always see what's vulnerable and trembling, and she probably knows that, because she sits right behind the driver. I skip that seat to save it for another fifth grader, Ralphie, who is small and tender pick-ings, and gets on at the next stop. He has a hard time because his brother beats him up too. Us losers always look out for each other, but that's hard to do before knowing predator from prey.

Things we find out about Eleanor: the hand-me-downs are because a bunch of teenage sisters live in her house, unexpected noises make her scream real loud, and she cries during Animal Planet videos in class because she has a pet rabbit named Lucy. Coyotes can't resist tears and they are merciless to poor Eleanor. I feel real sorry for her, even though she draws them all, even Billy, away from me and Ralphie.

She cries more than I think anyone can, at first. Still, she is the only kid who visits the dollhouse.

I don't know how the dollhouse got there. It leans against the base of a wide old apple tree on the edge of the playground.

It smells strongly of cats, like my aunt's house, and is white as antlers. It looks kind of like it grew out of the root knuckles of the apple tree, almost by accident. It twists like grandma's fingers, but the spines and knobs come together to make something that looks like a dollhouse just the same, with an open door, windows, and a steeple roof. There is always a small animal rotting there, tufts of fur missing.

At first, Eleanor seems scared of it like the rest of us. The coyote girls - they move in packs too - say she wears pilgrim dresses and tell her she smells like Goodwill. The coyote boys throw gum in her hair or capless markers that leave green and black splotches on her clothes. She finds out quick that when the coyote boys are chasing her, to give her cooties or pull her pigtails, they won't come close to the dollhouse.

I feel sorry for her, watching her cower away from it, yet close enough to the dollhouse to keep back the bullies. But, even in her apple-root circle of safety, she is my shield. With her on the playground to taunt, the others leave me and Ralphie alone, content with slinging insults. They are held apart, Eleanor and the circling coyotes, but I know it won't last. The leaves in the schoolyard turn red and brown. The apples grow red and heavy on the boughs and coyotes are smart hunters.

She stops crying before the apples are ripe. Even when Billy pulls the wings off a fly during times-tables, Eleanor doesn't cry anymore. When he smashes it across her spelling test, she hands it in anyway, bug guts and red smeared across d.e.f.i.n.a.t.e.l.y, her face like a stone.

She spends every recess at the dollhouse, gets closer and closer. Just before the apples are ready, low enough to pull, I see her with her ear pressed against the attic window, like a mouth telling her secrets. The coyote girls avoid her. Maybe girl coyotes are smarter than boy coyotes.

When the apples fall, Billy starts his favourite game, seeing how many bruises and welts he can cause when the recess teacher isn't looking. Since Eleanor isn't as much fun any more, and, really, nobody is safe when the apples are ripe, Ralphie and I brace ourselves. When Billy gets Ralphie in the face with an apple, the recess teacher yells at us all about his bloody nose. Then she takes him to the nurse and us kids are alone on the playground. No one's surprised when Billy throws an apple at Eleanor. The other coyotes join the game and throw apples at the dollhouse, laughing and yipping.

Apples pelt the house with dull thuds, and Eleanor folds her body around it, protecting it. I think she'll start crying again, but she doesn't. The boys run out of ammunition. Red apples are scattered all around the dollhouse and Eleanor, but there aren't any more in easy reach.

Eleanor stands up.

The look she gives the coyote boys. All the color flows down out of her face, like she is horn, or bone. Her eyes and mouth look like the empty holes of the dollhouse. There are no tears at all. She walks forward.

Billy picks up a rock. The other coyotes pick up rocks too. I can see it happening: Eleanor isn't going to move or give in or duck. They are going to hit her with rocks while the teacher is gone with Ralphie. I can't let that happen.

I reach up and grab Billy's arm. 'Stop,' I say.

He pushes me down. I brace for a bunch of rocks, but Eleanor steps out from under the apple tree. She grips Billy's arm, lifts up on her tiptoes, and whispers in Billy's ear. Billy's head tilts toward her, as if to hear her better. None of us can hear anything but hissing. He makes a loud choking sound. He runs away from her, tears on his cheeks, barking sobs floating in the air behind him.

The coyote boys look at each other. Eleanor looks back at them, no expression at all on her blank-paper face. They drop their rocks and run. There is only me and Eleanor and a dead rabbit named Lucy under the drooping apple boughs. She holds her doll-like hand out to me, white, empty, and alone.

And I take it.

The coyotes leave us alone now, Ralphie, Eleanor, and me. None of us cry. We spend our time at the dollhouse, listening.

Revelation 2:17
M. Regan

Little Alice fell

D

O

W

N

the hOle,

Bumped her head

and bruised her soul.

0.

'Looking back, my pet,' she murmurs at the meal's end, 'the most inhuman thing about you has been your extraordinary reserve of patience.'

The comment is offered in lieu of gratitude, complementing the glance she casts the figure beside her. An elegant smear of a man, that figure attends with a servant's obsequiousness. Earlier that day It had acted as chef and patissier, before that It served as housekeeper and guard.

Later It will play judge and executioner.

The creature donned Its various roles with the ease It did Its human-suit, each re-imagined Self built upon the foundations of the former. Only small details remain in the aftermath: a smile lined with teeth, the faint scent of petrichor, a looseness about Its fingertips, dimpled flesh dangling from not-bone.

She remembers those fingertips first skirting the edge of a pentacle. How their pads had grown pruned with the blood of those who dragged her there.

Its hands still bear those wrinkles now. They are reminders.

The girl reminds It, 'We have nearly reached the end of our partnership, and I, the end of my life.'

'Indeed, Mistress.'

'Then am I correct in assuming,' she continues, 'that there are no more secrets between us?'

That which lurks in the dark of her soul, that stands in the pool of her shadow, assumes a scythe-smooth simper. A sanguineous ray of sunlight follows the sharp of that smirk, illuming an edge that may yet cleave away the creature's ears.

She has seen those ears disappear before. She has seen all of It disappear before, fading in and out of reality like the Cheshire. Here and gone, there and back. So many impossible things had been believed before breakfast; now that dinner is all but finished, there is nothing that seems unfeasible.

There are no miracles, only the inevitable.

'There have never been any secrets between us, Mistress,' the grinning thing coos. She might roll her eyes Heavenward if that did not feel like blasphemy.

'So you say, pet. But you are very good at lying.'

'I do not lie, Mistress. Those of my ilk only ever tell the truth.'

'What you tell is your *interpretation* of the truth,' she contends with a gesture of her dessert fork. Tines glitter when flicked.

Were it proper to do so, the creature may have shrugged.

'As is the way of mortals, Mistress. You charged that I blend in with those around me, did you not? Blend I did. In all ways sans patience, I fear. For this oversight, I offer my most sincere apology.'

'You needn't.'

Dismissive, the girl pokes placidly at the pomegranate skin which decorates her cake, the garnish peeled thinly enough from its membrane to have curled into a ringlet. It reminds her of a clock spring. Time rolls along...

'Though on the subject of such things,' she adds, pushing at that coil, 'I have been wondering something for a while.'

'Yes, Mistress?'

'How did you learn to act so very human?'

With a nudge, the crimson trimming tumbles over a precipice of chocolate, landing amidst the debris of piled seeds. They scatter. Her thoughts do in kind.

Hades and Persephone, Eve and a Serpent. There are stories in the kernels' wet gleam, warnings of doomed women and those who had sweetly fed them. Fruit lines her plate like headstones in a cemetery.

She wonders which is to be her grave while the one who fed her smiles.

'For many millennia, Mistress, I have observed the populace of this realm,' the creature explains, its reply wending like smoke from the depths of Its lungs. 'When I first stepped onto this rock, even the Bible was but a distant dream. I have watched civilizations rise, fall, then return to the ashes and dust from whence its populace first crawled. Of course, it did not take me nearly so long to realize that like attracts like. In order to obtain my desires, it was easiest to appeal to humans on their level.'

'You learned to camouflage yourself. Like a predecessor to chameleons,' the girl chuckles, reminded once more of the characters in Genesis. 'Your kind gives the whole reptilian class a bad name.'

'Perhaps. Though in my humble opinion, Mistress, the class

Mammalia is no better off for its inclusion of homo sapiens.'

'Mmm. We are two-faced monsters in our own way…'

A sigh wafts through pale forelocks; her utensil slips between the seams of her lips. Metal and enamel collide with a *click*, the tinny sound an acknowledgement of punctuation. An ellipsis follows. Then:

'What do you know of Jericho?'

If the suddenness of the inquisition startles It, the creature does not allow that surprise to manifest.

'I was there to watch the walls crumble, Mistress,' It answers honestly. Honeyed nostalgia beads upon the ribbon of Its voice, enriching the glow of harvest moon eyes. 'I was there to hear the armies scream and see the fires rage and smell the viscera as it washed the war-torn streets anew. It was *beautiful*. The expulsion of a soul from its body is not unlike any other form of human release. It is base and obscene. Essence spills everywhere. There is writhing, panting, begging unanswered. And there is such pleasure to be reaped when it ends.'

'You make it sound like quite the show,' the girl notes, leaning back in the embrace of her chair. Despite having recently come of age, she still looks like a child to the one who serves her. Though in fairness, all humans do. 'An orgy of grotesqueness, to be sure. And wouldn't the noblesse just eat that up…'

'They do have the stomach for it,' It agrees. 'I might even argue that there are those amongst the aristocracy more devilish than myself. But in the end, *I* would be the only one who relished the feast.'

'Oh… Perhaps not 'in the end."

Absently, the girl scrapes together the juicy innards of the pomegranate. The grate of cutlery over fine porcelain is irritatingly shrill. Perhaps that is the reason the beast's sneer grows taut, thinning to the point of brittleness.

Perhaps not.

'Whatever do you mean, Mistress?'

The girl hums, deftly skewering a single seed. 'I mean that vengeance can be served in a number of ways. You may like the taste of today's variant, but someday your supper call will be made on a ram's horn, and you will find the dish before you far less enjoyable.'

'Begging your forgiveness, but I still do not follow.'

'Then you should reread last night's bedtime story,' the Mistress retorts, bored. With a snap of her wrist, she sends the ruby seed soaring. A second kernel is flicked into the distance of the dining hall not a moment after, rejected for reasons known only to herself. 'If Jericho has taught us anything, it is that nothing lasts forever... Not even the walls that we build to protect ourselves. *Especially* those. External defences are weak enough. Internal ones are weaker still. And with all that you've endured, my pet, all of the angry, agonized souls you've allowed to circle your insides, I imagine the only thing you're waiting for is 'a great shout.' After that, your walls will topple and you will burn. Or shatter, maybe, like the precarious Humpty Dumpty. You will wake to yourself and the Wonderland you know will fall apart.'

There is gravity in the pronouncement. The pull of it is enough to see the beast tip forward, stumbling, pitching...

Laughing.

Glee burbles, thick and black, through gaps in unsheathed incisors. Amusement melts down the creature's chin in rivulets of boiling molasses, the cracked abyss of Its maw shimmering with stalactite strands of saliva as It giggles in rebuttal, 'With *respect*, Mistress... I believe you have forgotten one very important fact.'

Another seed plummets through the air, vanishing beyond

the far end of the table. The creature's irises seep a similar hue, faceted like garnets in the haze of an encroaching twilight.

'Unlike Jericho, unlike *Adam*, unlike those who are descended from him, we demons are not made of mud. The 'walls' to which you allude are built of sturdier bricks. In construction, they are not as narrow or fantastical as those in your fairy tales. There is no way 'in,' I assure you. No cry loud enough to see me topple or to raze my defenses.'

The declaration is dotted by an aril bouncing off the creature's cheek. It stiffens, blinking. Its Mistress is the one grinning now.

'No?'

For an instant, her soul shines with intensity behind the windows of her eyes, as bright as the sunset that streams through stained glass. There is a warmth to its radiance, a near-physical heat. Like flames are said to leap, so too does the creature to attention.

The girl's own attention returns to her plate.

'You wear the mask of humanity so well,' she softly appraises. It sounds like flattery. It is not. 'Thinking back, perhaps that is the only thing about you that ever truly frightened me. I began to wonder if there was any real difference between us. After all, did we not both Fall from grace? Are we not both driven by the same urges? Have you not ever wondered if this mask will one day cease to come off, or worse still, prove to never have even been a mask? It is said that we are what we eat. As you prepare your dinner, do you not fear losing yourself to the role?'

'…you think I might lose to a dinner roll?'

The devil's genuine confusion catches Its Mistress off-guard, much as the would-be riddle has bemused It. Humour blusters through flared nostrils; chortles are pared into breathy wisps by bared teeth.

The last of the pomegranate kernels is pinched between her

fingers, held in the fashion of blessed wafers.

'And he took bread, gave thanks and broke it, and gave it to them, saying, 'This is my body given for you; do this in remembrance of me.'

Her gullet undulates as she gulps down the seed. Her stained hand does not tremble when it is offered.

In a final act of obedience, It takes the bread, gives thanks, and breaks it.

It has no plans to remember.

I.

To begin, there is the press of pliant lips.

A head lolls, the energy needed to hold it aloft already drained away. Spittle oozes enticingly from the slit of her mouth, the berry flesh having burst to openness. Juices sluice, pleasantly pulpy.

The contrasting colours of the corpse's shell and her insides seem to the creature a beautiful metaphor. Intoxicated by ecstasy, by anticipated satiation, It wonders if It might find Hell itself lurking at the bottom of her rabbit-hole throat. It would not be shocked, if so; dealing with her had certainly been hellish, at times. And would that not be convenient? To be led from one home to the next by way of a single fall?

If It but fell one more time…

Its own throat contracts around the musing, a pseudo-Adam's apple set to bobbing. It gulps again, this time around an elixir of *psyche* and *pneuma*, twenty one bitter grams of lachrymose filling Its belly.

Hunger remains.

So does *soma*.

II.

L'apéritif and *l'amuse-gueule, l'entrée* and *le plat.* Any meal worth savouring is a coursed affair, from those served to one's Mistress to the Last Supper of the Saviour. And if Christ himself saw reason to indulge Gluttony, surely a demon must do so the same.

The girl's corpse has been splayed across the dining table, her slender fingers woven and her lacy lashes low. She is an extravagant *piece de resistance* and oh, resist she had, the saucy thing. She had resisted everything good and decent in this world, all in the name of self-sought justice. How poetic. How foolish.

How lucky for It, the creature decides, for that vim and vinegar had spiced the Mistress's spirit most delectably, and having basted in baseness had turned her into quite a treat. That she had walked herself into the oven once just desserts were doled is the very icing on the cake. In fact, in that sense, she may well be considered the cake itself.

Upon a plinth of ornately carved mahogany, the cadaver waits like one of Alice's treats, having ordered its own consumption.

Eat Me.

If vaguely, the demon takes note of this second storybook allusion, reminded again of poetry and foolishness. Odd. It had never wasted Its own thoughts on such frivolity before; the girl had been the one to enjoy that brand of inanity. Or at least, she had shown more interest in the words of Lewis Carroll than she had in the Word of God, though they had perused both tomes with frequency.

He took the bread-and-butterfly and broke it, It thinks in echoes of her voice, *so that it might no longer flap its wings. This is my body given for you, so: I want you to Eat Me. I want you to Drink Me.*

Those who contract with devils always get what they want.

And in exchange, the devil gets what It wants.

It wants to eat.

A gown is shucked in the style of corn husks, undergarments peeled with the delicacy of apple skins. Ribbons are unwound, heels removed, and rings replaced by puckered lips. The beast's ravenous head slides past nail, joint, knuckle; soon, the tips of fingers and toes have been nibbled to nothingness.

It is with far less delicacy that fangs rupture the drum of her stomach. *Pop*, and a fairy ring of scarlet toadstools appear. They do not bloom so much as well beneath the curvature of her ribs, cousin to those mushrooms that grow from the marrow of the dead.

Mushrooms, butterflies. Caterpillars.

Who are you?

I Am That I Am.

When the devil next remembers to swallow, It cannot ignore the floral flavours souring Its tongue. Violets, tiger lilies, daises, larkspurs. There is a rosiness redolent of memories. Unbidden, visions pool behind the creature's eyes like blood in fingertips and bellybuttons: golden summer gardens, riddles shared and games of chess.

It blinks. It growls, encouraging Its belly to do the same.

It does not.

Yet, It feels empty.

III.

Christ rose after three days.

She decomposes instead.

With the devil assistance, the Mistress's carcass crumbles from its bones. One, two, three. A day is dedicated to flailing away each pellucid layer of skin: epidermis, dermis, hypodermis; whorls, folds, and ridges.

There is twisted reverence in how It plucks hairs from her nape, from her arms and legs and private places, to savour like pieces of candy floss. Canines sheathed, lest savage inclinations overwhelm It again, the creature suckles at tenderized flesh, trembling when the girl's confectionery coating disintegrates like sugar and snowflakes.

Eat Me. Eat me and you will not surely die, but...

The dining hall resounds with whispers of Eden's snakes, though chameleons are what It thinks about when membranes give way to muscles. Her colours change from white to red as Its acidic discharges reveal, then fray, then obliterate, twined ropes of ligaments. She falls apart around snapped strings.

One, two, three: *R-Ri-Riiiiip.*

Her mandible detaches itself, too heavy to be contained within a cocoon of cobwebbing. The curved bone wobbles, tumbles; it chatters against the knobs of a rib cage before settling against the lump of a groin.

The groan that echoes throughout the house's bowels shakes its very foundations.

Without a jaw to contain it, the corpse's tongue sags to freedom, cleaving cleanly through vestiges of tissue. It unfurls in parody of welcome. It lolls within tattered oesophageal film, the remains of that tube long and dark enough to fall through.

Rabbits and expressions about them circle within Its head. *Off with her head.* Off with her head in with Its own, for it would be a shame to let that satin-soft temptation go to waste.

Christ rose after three days.

The devil likewise.

IV.

Time and the beast have eaten the flesh from the girl's apple cheeks; her scalp is no more, and the grey, frail lids of her eyes have been pared. She is smooth, featureless. Expressionless.

This is natural. All of mortality is ephemeral, and every veneer wears away eventually. Mountains become boulders, become pebbles, become dust. This form will not last for long, either.

If Jericho has taught us anything, dear, it is that nothing lasts forever.

Another second passes. Second lives and second chances. Second thoughts.

Beneath the orts of the girl's sinew, there is the frame that gives her shape. Tendons come apart like decayed gristle; her body sloughs free of residual muscle, shedding what little is left like a serpent.

Again there is the memory of a garden, stirred by the rattle of a pomegranate seed. She had not digested it in full.

It does not feel full.

An unknown sensation is gnawing at the creature's stomach, Its innards tingling as if with sepsis. The ichor in Its ancient veins has curdled. Its sense of self has warped, twisting so that instincts and desires no longer align as they ought. As they should. Thoughts butt futilely against one another, like puzzle pieces with shaved corners. Like cornerstones that had fractured.

In the distance, It imagines It can hear the sound of limestone toppling. Porcelain. Bone china.

The nerves threaded through the Mistress's spine have become little more than spider strands. Her vertebrae are chattering beads upon that chain. They fall to the floor when something within snaps.

Something within has definitely snapped.

It wonders if It is going mad.

V.

There are two hundred and six bones in the adult human body.

Two hundred and six cogs, wheels, and glass-fragile sprockets that - when meshed together - create mankind's most basic piece of equipment. And while the skeleton upon the mouldered table had only just matured, the meticulous devil is indeed able to count to two hundred and six on fingers, toes, and sundry shards.

It checks the number twice, thrice, four times. It spreads Its Mistress out, grouping fragments into piles: humerus, radius, ulna, trapezium, sacrum, ribs, coccyx, patella, tibia, tarsal, calcaneus, talus…

The girl's petite stapes reminds the beast of the wishbones It had carved from turkey dinners, of how she would roll her eyes when they were given to her for play. Citing childishness, she would decline the gift, but in the dead of night the creature would find them halved upon her writing desk, their shafts ivory in the moonlight.

It was a discovery that always made the beast chuckle. Smirking, It would consider the many terrible things that would have to break in order for her wish to come true.

Now that it has, It is no longer smirking.

VI.

There is honesty in a body deconstructed. Reduced to pieces and parts, stripped of pretexts and pretence, the haughty Mistress no longer has anything to hide behind. No airs, no lies; no skin or fat or muscles. There is nothing here but the bare-boned truth, for that is what she has become. That is all that is left:

Truth and bare bones.

When It wets Its lips, the devil still tastes the nectar of her marrow, corrosively sweet. A serpentine tongue searches out what life yet lingers within the calcareous craquelure of her femur, as if that pittance will somehow accomplish what the rest of Its meal had not. Once a terrifying beast, the devil has become a lapdog, complete with a bone in Its mouth. Oh, how the mighty have fallen…

Did we not both Fall from grace?

The demon knows of falling. It has done so before, Its scorched essence leaving streaks across the sky. It had toppled down and down and down, plummeting from Heaven like a pomegranate seed.

No, like Alice.

No, like a star.

Yes, like a star, and It had made a wish upon Itself that day. It had wished upon whatever remained of Its heart, much as mortals would soon be making wishes upon It: An innocent prelude to innocence lost. Too lost to be guided home, however vibrant the constellations. However stable.

It is not stability that the longing look for in the void.

And so it was that man and monster fell together: End over end, beginning over beginning, bumping heads and bruising souls as they plunged from moral high grounds to the Pits waiting below. The passing of eons had seen that journey become familiar to the creature. No longer does recalling Its first descent frighten the former angel.

But the fall to Its knees now does.

Humpty Dumpty sat on a wall.

Somehow, this fall is more terrifying than the first had ever been.

Humpty Dumpty had a great…

Because this is a different sort of falling.

I'm afraid I can't explain myself, sir.

This is a different sort of…

Because I am not myself, you see?

This is a different…

But if I'm not the same, the next question is,
This is…
'Who in the world am I?'

VII.

The devil cries out, something within Itself cracking. Shattering. The agony of Its howl resonates like the blare of a horn.
And the walls come tumbling down.

∞

Ashes to ashes. Dust to dust.

The creature sits primly, ankles laced and eyes dull with a skull in the centre of Its lap. Like the head of a sleeping child, It strokes the length of the Mistress's temple, quiet as It yearns. As It prays. It is a temple after all, for now there is no better place to worship, though someday that bone will fester back into the mud from whence it came.

It is an inevitability that the demon suddenly cannot bear.

Distantly, there is the thought of entombing her grains within glass, of passing time with her in a new and more literal fashion. But there is only one ossuary in which It wants to see her rot, if rot she must, and it is not one made of traditional walls. How stupid it would be to try and protect her thus, when walls never stand forever.

'How long is forever?' asked Alice.

'Sometimes, just one second,' replied the White Rabbit.

Sometimes, it is just that. Sometimes, it is far longer.

He took bread, gave thanks and broke it, and gave it to them, saying, 'This is my body given for you; do this in remembrance of me.'

It is a poor sort of memory that only works backwards, but

with deftness, the creature does as Its poor memory instructs: It plucks crumbs of Its Mistress from the stagnant air, much as the doomed might pick a pomegranate from a tree.

Motes dance, swirled about in what phantasmagorical radiance still pours through smoggy stained glass. Terrified of feeling emptier than It already does, the demon stuffs her smallest specks into Its mouth, choking them down before they can float back up to Heaven. Or, God forbid, before they can amalgamate again into clay.

Once upon a time, the Mistress had gifted her servant a name. Once upon a time before that, a man who had shared that name placed a curse upon devoted earth: Should anyone be imprudent enough to try and rebuild Jericho, they would pay a dear price.

That was the Lord's will. That was His wish. And when the Lord makes a wish, He spares nothing to see it come true.

No one is spared. Not even the stars.

I knew who I was this morning, but I've changed a few times since then.

Fragmented Words of God and Lewis Carroll come apart around Its ears. It dares not try and put them - or anything else - back together.

Alone in a crumbling manor, Joshua sits and thinks of broken things.

19 December, 1863. I mark this day with a white stone.
Reverend Charles Dodgson

Eleanor
Lisa DeYoung

The crisp brown leaves piled up in front of me but didn't completely hinder my view of the old, deteriorating house. The house was ugly, hideous. The layers of grey paint peeling off the sides hung in bulky strips. Grey and black shingles covered the ground, leaving several holes in the roof. The porch was rotten and sagging, missing several floorboards. Termite holes peppered the railings and the rusted porch-swing hung haphazardly by a single chain still bolted to the ceiling. The property sprawled over three acres and butted up to a dense, unwelcoming forest. The lilies that grew in the front yard in the summer were the only thing of beauty on the entire place. The sea of boisterous orange and yellow would blanket the lawn making the grass practically invisible. Paul had wanted to get rid of them, he said they were unruly and took over the lawn. I convinced him to keep them. I loved them, they were so beautiful and made me smile even after Paul ceased to. His smile was what stole my heart the very first time I saw him. I did miss it, on the days that I forgave him, that beautiful comforting grin that graced the lips of the man I loved. I'd loved him passionately, more than I'd ever loved anyone. I still loved him. He'd loved me too and once told me that I was the only woman he had ever loved; that he could ever love. We were so happy together. Then suddenly, we weren't.

A single long black hair pulled from the collar of my white robe one cold October night sent my entire world spinning and changed my life forever. I can't recall exactly what I said; all I knew was that Paul had broken my heart and that her name was Joyce. I remember how I tried to explain my point of view and how he would only hear his own. After hours and hours of arguing I crumbled into a sobbing pile on the mouldering grey carpet of his bedroom floor, still clutching the dark hair in my hand and he indicated that I should leave without even speaking. I had never known pain like that; like a dagger in my chest that I could not remove. I left the house against my will and promised myself one day I would return and she would be gone. I knew in the back of my mind that someday Paul would come for me and we would be together again. From that evening on I watched the house from the place where I hid and relived that day over and over in my mind…struggling desperately to purge his shameless secret from my memory, to forget the long dark hair and my conjured visions of its owner. I tried to focus only on Paul's sweet words and take solace in the sound of his voice that resonated in my memory…'The only one I could ever love… The only one I could ever love…The only one I could ever love.'

My throat felt full of gravel and my chest was thick with anger the first time I saw her sitting in the white Adirondack chair wrapped in my robe. All the effort I had taken over the previous two weeks to suppress the horrible memory of her existence was instantly wasted as the anger, disappointment and grief of Paul's betrayal flooded my mind. I'd wanted to scream at him, 'Who is she?! What is she doing in my house with you?!' But I couldn't speak. I couldn't reveal myself. I couldn't let him see me. It was horrible, horrible to watch them together, but I couldn't look away. I couldn't move. He kept looking over the top of his newspaper at her with those beautiful eyes that used to gaze at me. I'd imagined her to be a hideous, beastly woman with a weather worn face and an abysmal grin. After actually seeing her I couldn't deny the fact that she was beautiful. Long slender legs peeked out from the white terry-cloth robe and teased Paul's lustful gaze. Jet black hair cascaded down to her tiny waist in rolling curls. He was beautiful too. They were beautiful together. I hated them both. I watched them eat breakfast outside together every Sunday for two months. I watched and felt like I had been hit in the face with a fistful of nails. I couldn't help myself. I couldn't stop staring. The cold wind whipped into my soul as I watched them and hated her more and more each day. I didn't care how cold it got. I longed to see her, to over analyse her, to find some reason to hate her more than I already did. I wanted her to suffer. I wanted something awful to happen to her. I knew these were horrible thoughts but I couldn't help myself; she was with him and there was nothing I could do about it. So I just watched. Day after day I watched them. I wasn't sure if they could see me, see me seeing them from the place where I hid. I was sure they couldn't but slowly realised I didn't care if they did. Then as quickly as she had entered my life and ruined everything I had, she was gone.

Winter came and I watched the house fall further into disrepair. More shingles flew off the roof and skidded onto the melting snow to be lost in the muck of mud and dead leaves. Bricks crumbled off the chimney and thudded to the ground and a family of raccoons made their way into a gaping hole on the west side of the house. The ice that accumulated on the windows made it difficult to see into the living room any more but I could make out Paul's silhouette pacing the floor from time to time. She wasn't there. I couldn't see the expression on his face but I could see him wringing his hands together as he paced. I wondered what was wrong and wished I could run to him and tell him I understood, that I forgave him. Sometimes I would see him sitting on the deck, alone, shivering, wrapped in a tattered blue blanket looking out at the forest. I so desperately wanted to be wrapped in that blanket with him, to put my head on his chest and hear his heart beat. I missed him so much. I wondered if he missed me too. I'd almost completely forgotten about Joyce. I was curious to know what had happened to her, where she'd gone and what she was doing, but I was glad she hadn't been back. Perhaps she'd broken his heart and moved on to another victim; perhaps he had done the same to her. Joyfully I thought how wonderful it would be if he had broken her heart, if she'd suffered the same pain as I had. I imagined her dejected and sobbing on the rotting grey carpet of his bedroom floor, pleading with him to let her stay, and he asking her to leave without saying a word. Perhaps I was the other woman this time and now Paul would come for me. I could only hope, hope that he'd come to me and tell me that he'd been wrong, that he would kneel down and look into my eyes and flash that wonderful smile of his and tell me we could be together again. And I would forgive him. I knew I would forgive him. I already had forgiven him. He hadn't meant what he'd done. He hadn't meant to drive me away. He loved me. '…More than any other woman ever.'

On the first day of spring Paul stepped off the deck into the back yard. He carried a ragged grey blanket in his arms and there was a look of confusion and concern on his face. He clumsily stepped over the fallen shingles and kicked the pieces of crumbled brick to the side with his boot. He was headed my way. This was it. He was coming to apologize. I knew it.

I knew this day would come. I knew if I were patient enough and forgot about her that one day he would return. I wanted to cry, I wanted to scream his name and run into his arms but I couldn't move. His dark hair shone in the morning sun as he trudged through the dense forest behind the house. Sweat rolled off the tip of his nose and dripped onto his grey flannel shirt. My chest felt as if it would explode in anticipation as he neared the place where I hid. What would I say when we were finally face to face? I couldn't say anything. He looked beautiful. I wanted to be with him so badly. Suddenly he was standing right in front of me. The horrible visions that had plagued my mind for so long vanished and all that remained were the wonderful memories of how in love we were. He had come back for me. He knelt down on the muddy forest floor in front of me and flashed me that wonderful smile. He was as beautiful as ever. He bent down and whispered, 'I'm sorry, Eleanor.' and laid Joyce's lifeless body down on the ground next to mine.

Body of Work
Simon Kewin

She was standing in the queue for coffee when she noticed him. Her feet ached. Water dripped off the canvas awnings in fat drops after the recent rain, turning the site of the book festival to mud. She turned around and there he was, some way behind her in the queue. He was dressed in a black leather jacket, a white tee-shirt underneath, a look she had always liked. His hair was unruly, as if he had run his hands through it once too often and it had stuck. He was very pale, like he was about to faint. He didn't see her, his attention caught in a book he cradled in crossed arms, like a baby. Something he read had amused him. He had a nice smile. She glanced back at him several times. He was definitely alone.

After the book signing she caught a glimpse of him in a corner of the busy tent, reading his now autographed copy of *Midnight's Children*. She hacked her way through the throng towards him, her own copy of the book deliberately visible in her hand.

'Crowded isn't it?' she said.

He looked up. There was a pause, his eyes taking a moment to focus upon her. He smiled, looked surprised at the same time.

'Yes.'

'Seeing anyone else?' she asked.

'Le Guin.'

'Oh really? Me too.' She lied effortlessly.

This time, as the summer rain came down again, they queued together.

I was seventeen when I first noticed the change. I was scratching a patch of dry skin on my chest when I became aware of how smooth, how cold and lifeless it was. I remember thinking that it felt just like paper, silky but hard. I remember smiling at the notion. I remember my smile fading soon afterwards.

I tried to ignore it at first. I told myself it was nothing; it was a phase; it would go away. Hormonal. But each day, when I lifted up my tee-shirt to check, I found the patch of dry skin was a little larger than the day before.

'Hi Russell.'

'Come in.'

His house was just as she had imagined it would be. One of the old, black-and-white houses found all over that corner of England. It leaned and it sagged, as if slowly deflating. The horizontal wooden beam that stretched above the windows and door was bent into the shape of an ox yoke.

Inside it was a mess. No, that wasn't fair, it was tidy enough, Spartan even. But it was filled with books. From gaudy novels to old hardbacks, their covers a faded red, like dried blood. They were arrayed in double rows on the bookshelves, piled in teeter-ing columns all around the floor like stalagmites, stacked up each side of the staircase leaving only a narrow channel. The air was thick with the dusty smell of paper. There could be no doubt that he lived alone.

'A lot of books,' she said.

He looked nervous, like a little boy caught in the act of something.

'Oh, you know, I can never throw any of them away.'

'I'm the same.'

'A glass of wine?'

'You read me like a book.'

It was a very bad joke. She was more on edge than she had realised. A quizzical look crossed his pale features, then he smiled.

'Red or white?'

She had the distinct impression that he was following instructions he had read on how to be a host.

'Red, please.'

She wandered around the room, stepping between frayed scarlet rugs that were laid directly on top of the stone flags. There were no photographs to be seen; the only ornament a small gold vase on his mantelpiece, like an urn for someone's ashes. In one corner of the room, a tendril of some creeping plant had found its way inside between a window frame and the wall. Now it hung in mid air, deciding where to go next. From the kitchen, she heard the *plunk* of a cork being pulled from its bottle. She smiled to herself. He'd obviously missed the bit about opening it to let it breathe.

She picked up a book, a copy of *Great Expectations*, and sat on his sagging, red sofa to flick through it whilst she waited.

As they ate he became quieter and quieter. She understood. They both knew where this was going. She wondered if he was still a virgin. Maybe. Depending on your definition of the word she was herself. She finished off her chocolate tart whilst he merely played with his. In truth, he had barely eaten at all.

'Dawn,' he said, when she had finished, 'I'd like to show you something.' His voice was a whisper.

'OK.'

She thought it was going to be a book, but he crossed back to the sofa and sat down, waiting for her.

She followed him. He didn't move. Up close, she could see that he was quivering very slightly.

She placed a hand on his.

'Hey, it's all right Russ. Whatever, it's OK.'

He paused for a moment more, then lifted his tee-shirt off, not looking at her. There was a crackling sound, like paper flexing. She was about to comment on it when the sight of his chest stopped her.

It was covered with closely packed writing. Tiny black letters in regular columns covered his skin, like a page from a broadsheet newspaper.

'When you said you were a writer I didn't think you meant this,' she heard herself say. 'It's beautiful but… they're tattoos?'

'Not really,' he replied. He turned to show her the side of his ribcage. 'It kind of explains here.'

She moved closer to look where he was pointing. There was the faintest smell of sweat mingled with the tang of ink. She began to read.

> After six months I began to write. I remember mixing the pot of glutinous, black ink with a matchstick, the smell of it sharp and sickly. I remember the perverse desire to drink from the bottle, to glug down the thick ink, stain my lips, tongue and throat with it until I gagged. I remember wondering whether all the ink would affect me in the end. Poison me.
>
> I had a steel-tipped lithographic pen, its nib long and sharp like the head-parts of a weevil. I still use it.

It made a noise like a small, gurgling pond-creature as it sucked up the ink, drinking until it was a bloated leech. I held the pin-fine point against my chest and began to write. I knew I had to push the nib in deep to make the letters permanent, drawing tiny cobweb scratches of blood, the pain sharp but brief. Because the pen was always moving on, it was bearable. In fact it felt wonderful. It took me an hour to write the title. *Body of Work*.

She broke off and glanced up at him. He still couldn't look at her.

'I don't understand,' she said. 'You write on your own skin?'

'It isn't skin any more,' he whispered. 'Feel.'

She touched his side gently. It was like vellum, very smooth but not soft like skin. It was too cold. Too unyielding. Up on his shoulders, she could see, it was rougher, something more like blotting paper, until, on his neck, he had normal skin. She didn't know what to say.

'Sometimes, when my skin is changing, bits come away,' he said. 'A whole leaf peels off.'

'And what's underneath?'

'Paper. Just more paper.'

'But… how?'

He just shrugged, the skin near his shoulders corrugating.

'Do you still feel pain? Bleed?'

'Yes. I'm more sensitive to heat but less to cold. If I'm cut deep enough, the blood runs. I thought at first I'd bleed ink, but that would just be stupid. Sometimes the paper tears and there's no blood. And then it heals up.'

'And the writing?'

'It's the story of my life. I'm catching up on being a boy over here on my left forearm whilst covering my adolescent years down my right thigh. I add current events onto my chest as they occur. I aim to fill the last patch of bare skin with the words *The End* on my very last day.'

He glanced at her, daring a smile. She had imagined lots of ways in which the evening would go. None of them had been like this.

'So, you're still changing?' she asked.

'Slowly. Hopefully my face will go last.'

The cold weight of disappointment filled her, burying under its rubble her previous excitement. If she was honest, she could have put up with a lot. He didn't have to be David Beckham. She *liked* bookish. But this? The word *freak* came to her.

'Here's the chapter I'm currently working on,' he said, enthusiasm clear in his voice. 'Across my chest. I started it when I got home that night.'

Not knowing what else to do, she carried on reading. There was a chapter there called, simply, *Dawn*.

> A new chapter. If I could, if such a thing was possible, I would start a whole new volume.
>
> I've always imagined that I'd fall in love slowly, over a period of weeks or months. If at all. Yet with Dawn the process took seconds. Perhaps less than a second. I was at a book festival. I hadn't spoken to anyone for hours. She talked to me and I looked up at her. That's all it took. Here was the woman I loved. I can't explain how I knew this, but I did. One life ended and a new one began. Just like that.

'I was up all night doing it.'

The image came to her of them in bed together. When their

bodies parted, her front was covered with the writing too; a mirror image of his life all over her.

'Russell I… I mean I'm not…'

She ran out of words to say. Neither of them spoke for a moment. The light had gone out of his face as he reached for his shirt.

They said brief goodbyes standing in his doorway. It wasn't even properly dark yet. She was turning away to leave when he stopped her.

'Here's that book.'

He held out *Great Expectations* to her. She hesitated for a moment, then reached out to take it. For a moment, they both had a hand on it, holding it there between them.

She walked past his house three times, more and more conscious of how she must look. She told herself, repeatedly, not to be so silly. She wasn't a girl any more. But each time she spoke, the drifts of dead leaves through which her feet ploughed told her to shush, and she carried on walking, clutching the book, her fingers turning slowly to ice.

Finally, angry at the cold, kicking the leaves aside, she marched up to his black wooden door and knocked.

It took him a long time to answer. She was about to give up when it swung open unexpectedly. He was thinner then ever, wearing only a scarlet dressing-gown. His eyes were shockingly red within his wan face.

'I brought your book back,' she said.

'You didn't need to.'

'I think I did.'

He shrugged, as if it was unimportant.

'Can I come in for a minute?' she asked. 'Please?'

He hesitated, then, relenting, stood aside.

Nothing had changed within except that, on a small stool next to the sofa was a jar of ink, a shaving mirror and a delicate silver pen that rested on a small mound of tissue paper. The paper was stained a purple-red colour, like the juice from blackberries.

'What are you writing?' she asked, as if he was merely scribbling in a notebook.

'Nothing.'

'May I see?'

'No.'

'Russell, please. I know I hurt you badly. I was… surprised, that's all. But I've come back. I wanted to come back.'

'No.'

'Please? I won't run away again.'

He smiled, without humour, and pulled his dressing-gown suddenly open, like Superman revealing his true self.

'OK then, Dawn,' he said. 'Read away.'

He had filled his entire chest and stomach with writing now. She could see the same word repeated there, over and over, running in regimented columns down his body.

She looked closer. The word was *agony*, written thousands and thousands of times upon his skin.

'Oh Russ. Why?'

'Didn't I explain?' he said, his voice rough with the strain. 'Don't you see? This is the story of my life. When the pages are full my life will be over. So I'm filling the pages. I'm getting to the end of the story as quickly as I can.'

She took his hand in hers.

'Come on,' she said. 'Let's go to bed.'

He was silent for a moment, shocked. She could feel his pulse beating distantly through the cold smoothness of his skin. He dared to look up into her eyes.

'Bed?' he said, as if he didn't know the word.

She nodded.

'But...'

'I know.'

'We'll have to wait until the ink is properly dry,' he whispered. 'I don't want to smudge.'

Afterwards, she made him turn over and lie on his stomach.

'I'll try not to hurt you,' she said.

'You won't.'

She took his pen and held it over the space he couldn't reach between his shoulder-blades.

Carefully, she began to write, cutting into his skin with each stroke. Tiny rivulets of blood ran from each incision. She dabbed gently at his wounds with a tissue, revealing the hard lines of her words.

'What are you writing?'

'A new volume.'

'Tell me what you write.'

'I'm calling it… *Dawn's Tale.*'

Dumpling's Pillar
Petra Kuppers

That day, I had dropped off my refrigerated messenger bag at the food coop, after my last bike run. It was such a heavy thing, and however I padded the strap, it chafed the spot between my breasts, and the edge of my neck. Sheila, my fellow food runner, had stared down at her phone.

'Toni, look. What's on the board is weird. It's not coming up here.'

We had looked together, each of us locked into our little screen jewels, hers bright pink, with lurid violet stripes, like the chevrons on her biking pants. My own phone was a bit older, grey, with fine asphalt dots, quite heavy in my pudgy hand. I did need to upgrade.

The list on the screen looked too familiar: this was the route I had tracked earlier that day. All these lunches had already been delivered, by my achy calves, my wheels clasping the street as I pumped myself along. But here the addresses refused to go away, their map icons crowding the screen. I had shrugged, even though I would have loved to have been able to help Sheila of the silky hair. But there was nothing I could do, and she was getting frustrated. I left her pressing buttons, refreshing the picture.

My lonely weekend began. At the station, I locked my bike

carefully, after choosing rack mates comparable in prize and age, so as to not attract looters.

People everywhere. All waiting. When I took out my ear buds, I heard the announcement, first in Norwegian, then in English. All the trains in Southern Norway were down, standing still, their massive engines cooling in the early fall sunshine. And that included my scenic ride to Bergen, over the mountains and through the troll passes, past glaciers and pewter colored lakes that drown all memory.

There was no outcry. In Oslo station, the tour groups stood a bit forlorn, waiting to be told which track to go to for the replacement bus. They waited for an hour, then slowly dispersed, some to hunt in the labyrinth for a bus, some to go back to their hotels, to see if there was still a bed there for the night ahead. I watched the tourists, sitting on my soft bag, with all my e-gear safely tucked in the middle, juicing my phone. It turned out that I would not use most of the chargers much longer. Soon, most would be garlands in old Christmas trees, slung like off-white offal into the green plastic branches.

That night, I just watched. The station speakers would crackle on, every so often, informing us that all trains were standing still, encouraging us to search for alternative transportation routes. I had nowhere particular to be. I was able to tap into the web for a bit longer, checked Facebook, looked for weekend emails, missives from far away.

'I am thinking of you.'

Nothing much appeared, and Facebook was a screaming riot of US election coverage. I clicked away the page. I would not see it again.

At one point, early in the night, I went outside to stretch my legs. I walked past a city planting, full of blue and purple violets. The flowers shivered in the black soil. I leaned over the bed, and heard the gurgle of the water spouts beneath the earth. The water flowed, bubbled, growled, and the roots danced in the pressure waves. Soon, they'd drown completely. Normally, a signal would tell the wider system of the malfunctioning water cut-off. But tonight, the water flushed on in never-ending spurts, and the violets moved in a last dance.

Alternatives. We were running out, now, you see. Those communication nodes that broke in the food map apps, then the trains, they were advance warning, canaries, but we didn't see it at the time. Instead, we made jokes about Norwegian trolls and underground destruction squads. But the spark that laid low the trains and watering systems and underground and bus arrival times, that spark or worm or virus crawled its way into the wider waves, too. Two days after the dancing flowers, the internet went dark.

So there I was, in the dark. Watching. I could not report on my nightly migrations on Facebook. I had nobody to tell my stories to. All that was left were tiny blips of connectivity. Local phone-to-phone chains. Decentralized, eroding and low-grade

From that point on, when I took my charged phone out, I learned to look for a different little icon, a stylized phone rather than the bar fan. And if I saw it, I could hunt for the password. It might be hidden in a graffiti tag, plastered like chewing gum on a waste-paper basket, or written each new hour in chalk on the damp pavement. Somewhere, the magical list of numbers and letters would jumble out at the diligent searcher. Then I could reach my hand into a new thicket of electronic tracks, get a little touch crack. I could post a low-res image, or a snippet of text. Someone nearby, in the same lo-fi web, might reply. We each might look around, see if someone else was typing. These phone nets were very local. The old anonymity of the web was gone, but a new stranger contact world was being born, right there.

Let's go hunting, my friend. Let's go and search for connection.

The evening was drawing down, filaments of smoke and exhalation shifted in color bands over the fjord. The opera house still gleamed prismatic on the harbor. Next to it, the crumpled steel and glass flame in the water was hung with the debris of a new world: mobile phones, hung on their charger strings across the glistening facets, like drippy mourning stones, or black spaghetti.

I still held on to my phone, of course, my access point to the low-fi world.

There was Kristin. I recognized her coming out of our favorite Ethiopian at Gronland Station. Some restaurants were still working, while supply chains trundled out and the warehouses got depleted. People kept warning about food shortages here in Norway. As a food messenger, I knew how quick the balance could shift, out back, in the kitchens, with empty fridges, empty bags, all in the blink of an eye. But there was a good stock of lentils, and while the menu was getting smaller, we were not in the cellar yet.

Kristin jogged over, her cool fingers wrapped around the take-out container with its injera, hot lentils and Berbere sauce. She usually shared, if I wheedled up to her just right. I had bartering goods, too, fried onions, some sausage ends, from the Turkish baker in my neighbourhood. There were still neighbourhoods, even though most of the tourists trapped in Oslo roamed the streets at night.

Between the two of us, that was a full meal. We greeted each other, our take-out containers held at an angle, intentions clear, no threat. Like urban dogs on two legs, we ran through the protocol. Our little habits had already become quite ingrained, only a few weeks after the catastrophe. It did not take long for safety rituals to assert themselves, and we women were always good at working out fast solutions. After the circling, she initiated, took off her outermost jacket, and placed it on the ground, like an old-school picnic blanket but more dusty, army-green like urban paint warfare scenes. We were Mad Max survivors. But in the end, we both managed to sit down next to one another, and opened our cartons, and shared the food. Good.

Kristin was the blonde leggy one to my small dark dumpling. No boobs to speak of, but hair like sunshine, and violet eyes. Really violet, like vampires and werewolves. I would have given her my blood, but she had not asked for it. She was funny, too, and hard-core. Edgy, otherwise she would have hung her mobile on the harbour sculpture, too, and joined the wailing. No, not her, not me.

Remember when we were all into Pokemon Go? Competition for gym dominance, elaborate dragons at our beck and throw? She had that edge, the look that meant that she's sizing up what to take on, at what to throw the ball.

I wasn't that much to look at. Short legs, stubby arms, torso too long for my arms. No waist at all, hip tires enough to outfit a Jeep. But I had my own edge. I soldiered, marched, shifted forward tanker mode, whatever you did to me, whatever dyke names you threw my way. All systems go, and it was hard to stop me marching once I was on the move. So in some ways I could see why Kristin hooked up with me, at nights, to share food and go lo-fi-ing together in sketchy neighborhoods. I didn't think any of us would live very long. So we made it count, blonde sweets and chocolate tank.

We ate the lentils with elegant handfuls of the sour bread. Likewise, the onions and sausage ends. It was filling, and I loved the feeling of injera in my right hand, the way it stuck gently to my fingertips, a cool warm caress, soft and gentle. There I was again, munching and dreaming. Kristin knew it, of course, and ribbed me, teased me with her side-eye and eyelashes. I knew we both loved it.

Then it was time to cruise. We clicked open our phones, screen lights turned way low so to preserve the juice. We still had plenty of electricity in Oslo, but we've heard about lights out in the far country, whole swathes of country going dark at curfew. We were good at this. But what we did drained the phones, and we wanted to keep at it for a few hours, at least, without having to suck at the e-teat. Also, dimmer was safer. We did not know who exactly was out hunting at night, hunting for more than poetry snippets.

Kristin found it first – a well, a wide open network. 'Lana Net' was the name that came up, and the name whispered old movies and shapely hips in its swing. A few minutes of hunting about, and I found the entry code. It was stenciled small and tight into the neckline of a plunging bosom painted on the old roller-skating ring. Two boobs, no head, just a Victoria's Secret tight stack. The numbers and letters were in the white lace edging the blue bra. Nice one.

We hooked in. Flash. A stream gurgled into my Samsung, her iPhone. This was an active hole, a full well of sensation. We took turns reading out what scrolled over the tiny screens.

'Touch me now.'

'Your feathers are silky tonight, my dove.'

'I am in Venice, velvet mask pressed to my skin, patchouli.'

'I am looking for Daliah. 5'10", dark skin, tattoo of a night-lily on her left bicep. Seen?'

'See the pillar rising.'

'See the pillar rising.'

'I see the pillar.'

'Be my altar, pillar.'

Ok, there seemed to be a theme here. Kristin and I agreed to look for the pillar. What could that be, around there? We were in a spacious concrete neighbourhood, the back alley of tourist stores near the city centre train station. Some trash containers on the left. The skater ring straight ahead. An avenue of city trees to our right, angling away from us. Was that a likely site for worshipping pillars? We investigated in that direction.

This was not as easy as it sounds. The park angled beneath the city surface. It was built into the hillside. We'd had to go down, and it was dark in there. In the before-time, street folk assembled around there. In the centre of the park, there was a spoke of meeting lanes, and a circular bench. Not an easy or safe space for women to go hunting for pillars at night. But the rules had changed. Leaves crunched under our boots as we descended the slope, phones in hand. Where was this pillar?

Soon, we were at the central circular space. Leaves had drifted into patterns, herringbones over paving stones. Many of the city buildings around us were dark at night. Windows grinned at us with Halloween teeth. It was not quite pitch dark, but we knew that those street lights might not come up again. The leaves rustled beneath our feet. We couldn't see anybody around, not homeless, not player.

We stood in the circle, backs to each other, turning clockwise, scanning. There. The messages seemed to load quicker to the West. We moved that way, eyes half on the screen, half on the path ahead. The trees around us were coppiced, and bulbous gnarls had bled their strength into wooden canker fists. We nodded to each other - these were pillars more than trees. This was it. We moved closer. Kristin palpated the bark of one of the old ones. Rough, map tracks she couldn't quite read, like a blown-up fingerprint. She shook her head, moved on. I hung back a bit, tried to keep an eye out for company. Then, she beckoned me closer.

'Dumpling, look at this.'

Did I mention that she had a strange sense of affection? I joined her by the twisted tree stump. She took my hand. I tingled all over, but I did let her guide my hand to where she wanted to go. She smirked at me.

Then I touched it.

It was warm, glowing in the tree's old stone feel. We each traced the bark area with our fingers, and found a big circle. As clear an invitation as any. This was the pillar. And somewhere behind that, there was a party.

We sat down for a bit, checked the traffic. It had gone steamy fast.

'I lick the salt.'

'I lick the pepper.'

'I lick strawberries on the young masquer's belly.'

'Let me pepper you, all right.'

'Flowers of clove buds, my darling.'

'Salt lattice, to chain you on.'

'Sugar crystals to rub into your wounds.'

Weird. Kristin was intrigued, I could see it. She liked the baroque ones, the scene play, remnants of the cosplayers we each had observer-stalked in Vinland Park at weekends. We had told each other this as secrets, marking our bond. Now it was coming back to bite me.

She really wanted to go in. I tried to reason with her. Got nowhere. Because where was there to go when we both knew that food would run out soon, and that it was all doomed, anyway? So yeah. We agreed to go.

'You have to let it come to you.'

Ok. Sure. I tried to tune in. She was good at this. I could see the little blue veins in her small hand. That's how blonde she was. The hand rested against the warm tree circle, touching, stroking, and I could feel it. Full on. I hoped the tree had a good time.

It seemed that it did. The warm circle receded, shifted into the tree stump. Kristin stepped closer to the tree, and bent forward, into the open hole. I could have screamed with terror. But I did not. Instead, I crowded near, as I couldn't imagine my stroking hands having the same effect on the tree. So I made sure to ride Kristin's coattails. I put my hands on where her coattails would be, got an impatient swish for my efforts. But also a giggle. Good.

She pushed herself up some more, and glided in. I just went and did the same stupid thing. Up, over, down. We were belly-down, riding a smooth wood tube. If I had been three years younger, I likely would have been screaming with laughter. Instead, I was terrified. But she was up ahead, and she was banking, using her arms and hands to align in the tunnel, to twist up or down with the turns. I had no idea how deep we were, but we were riding this.

A bump. She was out. I was out. We were in a feather bed. Or something duvet-like, comfortable, warm, soft. We each scrambled out of the way, off, for it was also pitch black down here. Where were we? I reached for Kristin's hand. She did not withdraw it, and our fingers interlinked. It was electric, pink fire, velvet.

We pulled out our phones. Dialled up the light a little bit. Now they were flashlights, too. The Lana conversation was hot and heavy, and flew across our screens, like a randy chat-room scene, but more stilted, no swearwords, heavy on the romantic. Old emo, maybe. Who were these dudes or dudettes?

We rounded a bend in the tunnel. Now we could see light.

Straight ahead. It was hard to see what it was. There were refractions, shimmerings, mirrors in mirrors. There was a lake down there, and a crystal island, and a crystal forest, and a disco ball ruled over it. Candle light, at least that's what it looked like to me then, flickering and unsteady. The light was caught and thrown into the water, shifted into the lattices of quartz crystals, jewel lights and watery wavy reflections against white limestone. It was like a ballroom down there.

Kristin was enchanted. We tucked the phone away, and approached. There were figures. As we got near, they became clearer, three, no, four, one higher up on the shore of this cave lake, three on the island. They stood still, but they looked like sprung coils, ready to bolt. They were wary. Kristin did not care.

'Lana Tribe!'

She sang out. I tried to hush her, to play it down a bit. I could imagine so many scenarios in which this was such a bad idea. She did not look back, rushed down. My hand was still entwined with hers, so I followed.

The dude on the shore of the cave lake sure seemed cool. Queer, I got the vibe strong and clear. I relaxed far in my backbone. He was family, brown skin, black hair, pomade, hipster outfit circa 1970 reimagined as urban chic. He smiled at exuberant Kristin.

'Welcome to the Lana Tribe!' He shouted, his frequency similar to Kristin's, just one octave lower. They were full of glee, the two, like brother and sister at play.

I tried to look over to the lake island, to the three figures there, but I was having a hard time seeing them clearly. Who were they? What were they? Glee dude told us he was the ferryman, and to step right in. He handed over cushions, too.

'Get comfy, kids, I'll get you over!'

We stepped in. His hand was out, and it felt like really bad karma not to cross his palm. Whatever that meant. I dug deep in my pockets, and found a few sausage links from the Turkish baker. I arced a querying eyebrow. Would that do? That would do. He seemed well satisfied. We settled, and he poled the boat into the lake and toward the centre island.

Soon, we had covered the distance. The water lapped black at the boat, but the walls kept throwing light at us, skipping over the waves we were creating as our craft zipped forward. The island was really close now. It was made out of large quartz crystals, all sharp edges and mirror surfaces, octagons and long lances of white. I wasn't sure how one could step onto these without slipping, and I really didn't want to slip into these black waters. All the light stopped short down there, and no hint of what lay below escaped the surface.

Then, a small bump. We had arrived. Our guide hadn't said a word the whole time he'd been punting us over, and he was silent now, all glee now coiled. His eyes showed the way - over there, over the white expanse of sharp broken edges. Over to the three shapes, still indistinct.

The people there freaked me out. Was that fur on their bodies? Why was there this halo all around them? Where were the others? The lo-fi traffic was intense, and yet none of these people seemed to be working on phones. They were just stand-ing there. No. They were turning, like one, turning to face us. I knew I did not want to see them straight on. But then they were facing us.

I tried to step back, but there was Kristin, of course, pulling on my arm, nearly pulling the sleeves off me in her eagerness to get there, to connect. I tried to get her attention, to comment on the freaky scene that was going on, but she just galloped over the sharp translucent landscape, up and over to the three silent figures.

I followed as best as I could without twisting my ankles. We arrived. The crystal forest became a pebbled circle here, small round quartz stones of all hues, lavender for amethyst, yellow for citrine, all dusky and shaded in the half-light of the cave. Where was the light coming from? The figures in the centre of the circle seemed to be lit themselves. I could see them better now.

That was not fur, all over them, neither was it a halo. It was light-emitting, and bristly. It reminded me of the old toys of my childhood: fiber optic half-globes, glowing in all colors and twirling. That's what these people looked like, as if tiny bristles of fibreglass stuck out of them all over, prismatic lights at the edges, shining outwards. It was mesmerizing, and the closer we came, the more amazingly the colours glowed, twirled, ran over them like furry caterpillars.

Beneath the fur, the figures were pastel shades. I could see a face green as if a disco diva had dusted it down with her eye-shadow. Another brow looked purple, over there, a red hand, gleaming under the light bristles. They were androgynous, hair-less apart from the bristles, mixed, black, white, Asian, with strange twistings in their fingers, and long ropy bands over their forearms like scarification tattoos. I thought of lava lamps. I might have said that out loud: Kristin pushed me gently, as if admonishing me. I shut up.

'Are you the Lana tribe?'

Really? That was Kristin's first question? Here we were, finding some strange alien, human creatures under the earth, on a crystal lake, and she asked questions like a Survivor castaway. I tried to chuckle, but the sounds stuck in my craw. Kristin's question echoed over the lake, asked again and again, her voice shifting pitch as the crystals around us vibrated as if in answer.

No sound from the strange ones. Or was there? Kristin

hushed me. I wasn't making a sound, anyway. The echo died down, eventually, but there was a tone in the air now, like a hum, or a bell. The tone didn't die, but rose, shimmering like the light in the cave, rose again, got bigger rather than louder, and then it was in my head, and I wasn't sure if I was hearing with my ears or my teeth, my bones, my sinuses.

Wow. OK. Enough. I could see Kristin suffering next to me, not sure where to put her hands to block the escalating sound-wave. Then it was over. Quiet.

A gentle fall of drops somewhere in the cave, so loud in the hollow left by the departing crystal wave. Some strange chitterings. Mice? Spiders? I thought spiders, probably the thing that could scare me most down here: big furry hard-carapaced spiders with eight eyes staring at me.

The three light folk shifted position in the crystal ball circle, and now I could see where the chittering was coming from. It had probably been there the whole time, but our ears had needed a tune-up to hear it. It was a familiar sound, actually. Behind the light people, ten or so crystals reached high up, like beams, or prison bars: white, translucent, terribly sharp at the edges. These were the pillars. Behind the crystal pillars, I could see a bunch of youngsters, just like Kristin and me, kids with parkas and colourful leggings, some with wrapped feet, some with sneakers, all typing away at their phones. This was the Lana tribe, not the light creatures with their fibre-optic fur.

Down there, in the cave that did not freeze, in the blood-letting of the crystal grid, this tribe stayed in their gym, their castle, their stronghold. Long wires looped from the phones to the crystal pillars. The wires were not black, like the chargers that looped at the opera house. These were white, virginal white, much whiter than Apple's charging cords. Blindingly white, glowing milk lapping out of the matrix into the machines.

The kids were typing, their fingers glowing rosy and maroon, depending on skin colour, little dots of red-tinged light hovering over the tiny screens. They sat hunched beyond the crystal pillars. Backs shaped into Cs, into coils of spine power. The shoulders were relaxed, the heads bowed, drowsing. They seemed asleep, even, only fingertips awake to the juice. Maybe their eyeballs shifted with the changing charts and images on the screens. The chittering was the sound of their typing.

I did not want to see their eyeballs, I realized. I really didn't want to get closer, didn't want to jack into the pillar milk. So I pulled at Kristin, again. She stood still, for a second, but then she leaned forward, poised like a greyhound before the race.

She was so beautiful, my shimmery rose one, so tender. I felt the skin on the top of her hand, smooth and soft, freckles of summer sun still on the white flesh. I was crying. She turned one last time. Her hand came up to my face, touched my round red cheek, a goodbye in her eyes. This was the place of the soft laser-fighting ones, connected, milky sweet flow, hard on the keyboard, integrated spines. She would soon be hooking in there, between the crystals, before the food fights began, upstairs, above the cave, in the city. She was not crying. This was home for her.

I had delivered her here, safely, and that was my part of the story. I was the dumpling looking for remnants of Turkish food while there were still some trucks that shuttled back and forth. I would find a way to make a camp fire. No doubt I would find a bunch of others, greasy hair low over our brows, to defend against rat hordes and human gangs. She was already lost to me. Kristin stepped away like a crane, into the white.

Punt boy whistled behind me. It was time to leave.

Welcome
Jennifer McLean

The mornings are the strangest. Anne has learned a few phrases and can sign for things like hunger, but these people speak quickly, especially in the mornings, and it is hard to understand. The children, her new husband's young brothers and sisters, mill around grabbing at food and gulping milk while their mother fusses. Anne draws patterns in the frost on the inside of the windows until they clatter out of the door, first the father with his sandwiches in newspaper, then the children.

She is used to the sea air. The sweet smell of her mother's cooking, her father reading the newspaper, grim face broken by smiles when she sits down in the yellow warmth of the dining room. The three of them just so. Even now Anne imagines them this way.

She sits down at the table with her mother-in-law in the sudden silence. They smile at each other vaguely. The woman, Mary - Anne had had to repeat the pronunciation over and over, 'Mary' - is small and dark, and she moves so quietly among her family that she almost fades into the walls. Neatly dressed in a housecoat over a brown dress, her face a little collapsed. Anne has been here for four days and this is the first time she has seen Mary sitting down; she wonders if this is new, if they had help in the past. Anne mimes drinking at her husband's mother and receives a nod and a smile.

She swings the kettle over the fireplace. The house is always cold and the kitchen is the only place to be at this time of day. Where Anne sleeps, at the top of the house, it is so cold that on the first night she woke up in the pitch black with numb lips, and had to find her coat to put over her face. 'I will be at home here,' she tried to tell herself. The room seems huge to her: perhaps they avoid lighting fires to save fuel. She knows the room used to be her husband's because his boxing gloves hang on the back of the door. William had told her that his mother never liked it.

While the kettle boils she finds two cups and measures the tea carefully into the pot. There is only a little milk left, so she puts the majority in one cup and keeps a small amount for herself. She glances at Mary, who says something she doesn't understand, but her face looks approving so Anne carries on. When she hands the cup to Mary they nod at each other, then the older woman gestures at the pot on the stove. There is a little porridge left. Anne points to herself questioningly and receives another nod, so she puts the porridge in a bowl and sits back down.

'Good morning,' she tries.

'Good morning. How are you?' Mary says slowly.

'Good,' Anne says, 'good.'

She wonders if they have ever met a foreigner before. Before they married, William had told her, in the language he'd learned for her, though never really mastered, that the city had lots of immigrants and she would be welcome; that his cousin had married a Polish man and nobody had said anything, or at least not to her face; that his parents would love her. He had been so smart in his uniform next to the boys she knew, skinny in their patched clothing. William is confident, and kind. This is the family that made him. As she eats, she rolls that thought around her mind.

Anne washes up her bowl immediately. It gives her something to do. There are only a few books in the house, kept above the sofa in the back room, and she doesn't feel brave enough yet to try them. The three she brought with her, rescued from her mother's collection, are in her language, and she has resolved to avoid them for now, for William's sake. The first day she spent mostly in bed, but since then she has tried at least not to get in Mary's way and to clean up after herself.

When she turns around, Mary is putting on a woollen coat. She gestures at Anne with a string bag. Anne looks around, confused, but the woman picks up the empty milk bottle, shakes it, then points towards the door. Anne smiles and nods. Mary points again and says, 'You and me.'

'Yes,' Anne says.

Mary places a hand on her own belly and nods towards Anne. 'Good?'

Anne blushes. 'Yes,' she mutters. There isn't as much to show for it on her thin frame as Anne might have thought, but she knows that William explained in the letter he sent ahead of her. Mary has asked this question once every day so far, then left the issue alone - whether because of the language problem or because she is displeased, Anne isn't sure.

'Good.' They leave together.

This country is also at war. She can hardly believe it, but she knows it is true. The streets are untouched and the women she sees doing their shopping or chasing after children are healthy in Anne's opinion - thin, perhaps, but upright. When they get to the shop, Mary gives a list, her coupons and money to the old man behind the counter and the things are handed over quickly and without complaint.

The last item is a bag of sugar and the taste of her mother's baking is suddenly on her tongue. Anne has to hold on to the door frame. The old man stops and looks at her, so she smiles and goes outside. She takes deep breaths, the coal smoke bitter in her mouth. Rows and rows of houses. Women and children and older men left behind. She remembers rows of low walls and tumbled bricks where streets were flattened. She remembers the last winter, when she left school and went to the factory and her mother would go hungry to send her off with something in her stomach.

'Good?' Mary is next to her, holding the shopping bag.

Anne nods. Her face is beginning to hurt from all the smiling, but she fixes one back on. She is saved from going into the butcher by Mary handing her the shopping bag and directing her to a low wall, so she sits and spins the brass ring round and round on her finger.

He told her it would be safer away from the bombing. His mother would be there for her and the baby, when it came. He would - no choice, of course - rejoin the regiment and keep pushing the enemy out of her country, though Anne wonders if there will be anything left in their wake. William's face had been earnest, but it had struck her at that moment that this man whom she had married, this handsome man she had known for a few weeks before marrying on her fifteenth birthday, could tell her anything at all. What else could she do but believe him?

She watches Mary walk out of the butcher's and into the bakery next door.

'It will be over soon,' he'd told her. She made the sea crossing alone. The lights on the boat were off, which she had expected, but once out on the sea she'd vomited quietly in the dark, imagining hundreds of armed men waiting under the waves, missiles loaded into tubes, silently watching. She hadn't felt connected to the child until that moment, crouched in a corner, promising to herself, or the heavens, or whoever that she would keep the baby safe.

Anne is still sitting on the cold wall when Mary comes out of the bakery with a small pastry and hands it to her. She inhales and immediately bursts into tears.

The days go by more quickly as the weather warms and the children start talking to her. They had kept their distance but, as her body changes and she moves more slowly, she finds herself one day sitting at the kitchen table while two of the boys and a girl eat slices of bread.

'Are you hungry?' The girl, Ellen, is looking at her. She speaks clearly, though still with those strange clipped vowels they all use.

'No, thank you,' Anne says.

'How is it?' The girl mimes a large belly and Anne laughs. The boys stare, open-mouthed.

'Good, thank you.' It is becoming easier to speak. Not with anybody outside this house - she has wordlessly handed over lists in the shop a few times, but nothing beyond that.

'Did you and William…?' And she says something Anne doesn't recognise. Looking at her face, the girl stands up, puts a coat over her head like a cape, and walks solemnly down the kitchen. She stops by the stove, puts her hands in an attitude of prayer, and then makes an exaggerated kissing face. 'Married?' she says.

The boys are laughing now, too. 'Yes. Married,' Anne tries the word out.

Ellen comes over to the table and puts her hands under Anne's elbows, lifting her gently up. 'You and William. Married.' She offers Anne her arm and walks her up to the stove. Anne stands there a moment while the girl looks at her expectantly. 'How?' she prompts.

'Oh!' Anne turns around and assumes a serious expression. In her own language she says, 'Do you, William, take Anne to be your wife?' She turns back as though to the altar and says, 'I do,' in a girlish, nervous voice. She repeats the pantomime but changes her voice to a deeper one on, 'I do'.

Ellen is clapping and laughing along, but Anne sees her face fall a little as she looks past the boys. In the doorway is the father. He has not spoken a single word to Anne in all this time. While his wife has begun to fuss around Anne, especially encouraging her to eat more and rest as the pregnancy continues, he goes to work - too old to fight, though clearly not too old for long hours - comes home for dinner, then leaves again or retreats to the back room while the children chatter with their mother in the kitchen.

All three children begin clearing the table as their father watches. Anne tries to join in but Ellen shakes her head. It occurs to Anne that the girl is not much younger than her, though numbers are still a little confusing and the ages of the children not quite clear in her mind.

As she stands by the stove, keeping out of the way, she strokes her stomach and feels a jolt as the baby turns over. Almost in spite of herself, she laughs.

She thinks about her mother more and more, especially at night, cold even as summer grows. The house seems to breathe. The tall ceilings grow further away and she hears whistling, falling, weeping. There is salt in the air. The baby moves more in the early hours and Anne wonders if this means anything, if she will be kept awake all night once it is born, if it will be a boxer like its father. She imagines a boy. That was what William had said, that he hoped for a boy. He had been pleased from the first moment she haltingly mentioned that she thought something might have happened. A boy. Anne wonders if there is any way to tell. Perhaps her mother might have known. In his letters, one or two per month, William jokingly talks about 'William junior'.

Her mother had had just the one baby. Or just the one living baby, she corrects herself. A draught rushes under the bed, the mist of her breath like steam. Her mother's eyes, sightless. The room seems open to the sky and Anne pulls the blankets over her head. Her father had been in bed when the bomb hit and it blew him to nothing, but her mother was in the kitchen, lighting the stove for the day, and they brought her out as Anne came home from a night shift. She has kept this image deep in her heart and not even William knew what she had seen, but as the baby grows in her, a terrible desire to scream grows with it. It bubbles up within her and she has to fight the urge to waken everyone in the house, to make them share in the terrible knowledge that your mother can look at you from a misshapen skull with her dead eyes.

In the grey light she knows that she is bleeding.

Anne does not tell anyone. How would she? Nothing else happens, for the rest of that night and into the morning, though the baby no longer moves inside her. She does not have the language to tell Mary, and only one of every three letters seems to reach William.

She is sure that Mary would understand. Perhaps this is normal. Perhaps Mary could tell her that: with each one of her several children, she feared it had died. Anne does not really believe this, but Mary's efficient silence is calming, and Anne becomes her shadow in every daily task. They wash clothing together, their hands mingling in the warm water. She wonders if she taints it. What kind of woman is she? It must be something she did: the days she spent hungry before coming here, or some mystery that other women know from their mothers.

They are wringing the clothes out when Ellen comes in. Her boots shed mud onto the floor and Mary begins to protest, but Ellen runs to the radio and switches it on.

Anne can only watch their faces, the crackle of unfamiliar voices moving too quickly for her to grasp. At first mother and daughter stand, staring at the radio as though at a person speaking. Ellen's hair is damp with sweat and she is still wearing her coat, but her hands are limp at her sides and she does not move. Without looking, Mary reaches for her daughter and clutches at her sleeve.

'What is it?' Their backs are to Anne and she has to ask again, so that they surface with a jolt.

'It's over,' Ellen says. 'The war is over.' She looks not pleased, nor relieved, but fierce, her shoulders back and her chin lifted.

At first, Anne can barely make sense of it. For one fragile moment she is walking through the door to her mother lighting the stove and calling her father for breakfast, but Mary turns to look at her and the spell is broken. 'William will be home,' she says, and his mother's eyes are full of tears. 'We are all safe.'

All three of them unroot from the floor and Anne is brought into their embrace, the suds from Mary's hands and the steam rising from Ellen's coat and the wash-water on Anne's dress smelling of the sea.

The street is mad with it. Children rush about unattended, doors and windows are flung open, and the women - more women, some older men - dress smartly if not flamboyantly.

Anne moves through them, smiling, catching sight of William's family occasionally. She keeps smiling. If she keeps smiling, the child will live. A cramping pain like a cruel hand moves through her body every so often, passing just as suddenly and leaving no trace, only the memory of itself. Anne keeps moving through the noise of a hundred families determinedly forgetting their losses.

Anne pauses as she finds herself back in front of the house. Home. Too tall for that, but it is William's home and she will grow to love it. She goes through the gate and through the front door. The late summer light is fading and the glow of the stove in the kitchen leads her on. Another cramp strikes, but she walks through it and on up the stairs, two flights, so steep she uses her hands like a child on the step in front of her. Into William's room, into his bed.

She tries not to cry out. The pain is terrible but beneath it lies fear, both for herself and her child, and she feels on the edge of shattering, like her father in his bed, floating away in the dust. The words come unbidden in her own tongue for the first time in weeks: 'Mother, mother, I need you.' All this time without her voice, holding herself together, and the pain undoes her. The noise continues outside and the room grows darker as Anne mutters to herself. An urgency fills her and it is a relief, to have a purpose. The child will live. She keeps smiling through the pain.

Without her noticing, the women are in the room, Mary and Ellen. Anne tugs at the blankets so that the girl will not see anything, but Ellen is as brisk as her mother and Anne falls back onto the pillows.

'I saw you leave,' the girl says.

'The baby... I think something is wrong.' She had meant to be alone, but Ellen looks at her steadily and Anne has the sensation of being tugged back in to shore by a strong hand.

'Mum, shall we get the doctor?'

'Too late, I think. Come on, girl. We'll look after you.' Mary lifts Anne's skirt and makes a noise.

'What is it?' Anne cranes to look but the pain comes again. Someone has banked up the fire so she can see the women moving around the room, and she is warmer than she has been in years. As a cheer rises outside, there is another wrenching in her belly and this time she screams.

She is coming apart. There is no other way to understand it, but if she can just hold on long enough, the child will live. William junior. She screams again and she is open to the sky, emptied out.

Mary and Ellen are still. The room is quiet, even the sounds of celebration calmer outside. The women look at each other, and again Anne is far away, left out of something they don't explain. Mary comes to the side of the bed and leans over Anne.

'William is coming home soon, do you understand me? He will be here.'

Anne tries to haul herself upright, to watch Ellen carrying the small bundle from the room, but she can barely move. Mary's voice reaches her through a mist. William. She licks at her lips and says the name out loud.

'William will be very sad.' Her mother-in-law's face is in front of hers, and Anne can see her choosing the words to be clear. Mary dips a cloth in warm water and wipes it gently across Anne's forehead; Anne reaches up to catch at the hand and for a moment they sit still, each holding the other's damp fingers.

'Things will be different now. William is a good, kind boy.' Mary withdraws her hand.

Her eyes are sightless. Mary's eyes. Her mother's eyes.

'He will be very sad, but this is for the best. I'm sorry.'

Anne struggles for the words to argue but all she can find is, 'No, no!' Not for the best. Her child is gone and William will be devastated. She tries to remember his last letter. When was that?

'Again. We will again.'

Mary looks straight through her. 'Not again. I'm sorry. He will try again, one day.' The woman stands up. 'It was a mistake. He is young. Everything is different now. My husband said we should have sent you home, but I thought it would be good to have the child. Now I can tell William that we did everything we could.'

The house seems to breathe. There are voices, not outside but in the room. Anne drifts, the pain fading.

'It was a girl, you know. I really am sorry.'

Her eyes. Sightless.

The Sleep Walker
Josh Jones

There aren't any children left in the village, other than Pasha and me, and Pasha won't play with me any more. He keeps to himself now, squirrelled away in some attic or wandering the surrounding wood in silence. Sometimes he'll happen upon me in the rowan grove, and I'll see the loneliness eating away at him from the inside out, leeching away his colour until his papery skin is almost translucent. We won't need to speak. He'll sit beside me, and we'll watch the birds flit back and forth between the branches. Other times he'll look for me between the wooden alleyways as I watch the villagers trudge to and from their shops and homes. But Pasha never follows me to the rail station, and I know he hates that I linger there, hates that I always seek a glimpse of a traveller or a flash of another child's face.

The trains arrive before dawn or after dusk, only stopping long enough to stoke the engines before chuffing away to larger towns. Whenever I hear the shriek of a whistle, I hurry to the station even though Pasha says I shouldn't. He says it's not good for me, that I should learn to find contentment. I tell him to stop being so bossy. Pasha has delicate, spindly limbs and never speaks above a reedy whisper, but he likes to act like he's the adult.

We used to play games together. He liked hide-and-seek best of all. He always knew the most clever of hiding places, but now he complains that I've found them all out. Now I'll sometimes creep up behind him and startle him, sending him scurrying from the shadows, his pale features colouring, his fists clenching in anger, and he'll shout at me, or as near a shout as he can make, more of a raspy choking whisper. *Zoe, leave me alone*, he'll say, and then he'll run away and sulk, and I won't see him for days and days, maybe longer. Time spins oddly for Pasha and I, and it's hard for me to remember how often we see one another or how long ago it was that I played with other children.

I like to sit atop the station house so that I can look inside each train car. Sometimes I'll see a motherly looking woman in one of the coaches, and I'll crane my head to search the compartment for signs of her family. Usually there is only an older man with her - perhaps an uncle, perhaps a new husband - or sometimes an old crone will sit by her and jab a gnarled finger at the darkness beyond the window. Only rarely will there be a child nestled beside her or curled in her lap, and I'll feel myself unmoored at the sight of such perfect skin, such cherubic and porcelain features, almost like I'm falling from some great distance.

I tell Pasha they remind me of dolls. I think I remember having a favourite dolly - I must have had one - but I can't recall her face, her feel, her smell. I ask Pasha if he remembers his old toys. He says nothing, just leads me into the attic of one of the abandoned cottages. Sunlight seeps through the slats and shingles of the roof. There, between two oaken beams, sits a small wooden box without a lid. He hunches beside it and motions for me to look. Inside, a miniature regiment of tin soldiers. Their paint has faded and their metal is burred in a layer of dust. I want to take them out, clean their faces and polish them until they gleam. One is missing a leg, another a rifle.

They're lovely, I tell Pasha.

Pasha doesn't respond, and I can't read his face.

Wedged against the side of the box, underneath a stiff-legged soldier, lies a faded daguerreotype. I make out a man and a woman, their faces stern, proud. The man in a silk suit, the woman in a calico print and bonnet. They seem familiar, like the fading vision of a dream I cannot hold on to.

Who are they?

Pasha shakes his head and stares at his hands, at his spidery fingers. Dust motes tumble about him in the splayed shafts of light.

Come, I have something to show you, I say.

He follows me out of the attic, out of the village and past the rowan grove, almost to the lake, still frozen in the final grasps of winter. A freshly fallen snow has blanketed the thinning wood. A hushed silence surrounds us, broken only by the crack of thawing ice that echoes across the lake. I lead Pasha into a small cleft that cascades toward the shoreline. A forlorn hemlock stump rises out of the snow in the middle of this ravine. It is burled and weathered with a fist-sized hollow in its heart.

Here, I say, and point to a reflective glint inside the darkened hollow.

He peers inside the hole, and his eyes widen. I love Pasha's eyes, how clear and pure they are, the colour of the sky reflected on the ice beyond us. He looks at me, then back at my collection, at the buttons, the ribbons, the cameos, and my favourite piece, the one that sits on top, the silver locket on a silver chain. I've never opened it, and I like to imagine what lies inside: perhaps a lock of hair, blonde or maybe red, curling just at the tips, and an ivory miniature of a young woman, her lips rouged and turning upward in maternal affection.

Zoe, where did you get these? Pasha asks, his words slow and measured.

I found them.

You took them.

No, they were given to me.

You took them from the Sleepers, didn't you. You stole them, he says, and his voice has risen to a shrill whisper.

They were presents. They gave them to me.

But Pasha doesn't listen. He never listens. He's gone before I finish speaking.

I kneel beside my collection and listen to the groaning ice. A spectral sun strains through a tear in the clouds, streaking them in shades of pink and gold. The edge of night bruises the low hanging sky. From the lake comes another plaintive wail, and I wait for the fall of dark.

I pace the roof of the station again, walking its length with my hands clasped behind me. I never lose my balance and am as silent as a cat. In the distance a whistle howls, moments later the train emerges from the shadows of the wood. It groans and hisses and finally halts beside the platform. The station master waves his lantern about and shouts at the carters to get moving, but these are old men, and they push their barrows forward with stooped and weary shoulders. I see the engineer get out and talk with the station master. A flask is passed between them, then a pipe is lit. Nobody else gets off, and I feel the tightening inside me relax. There will be no Sleepers tonight.

I do another turn along the length of the roof. The carters don't see me. They keep their eyes cast low as they unload the casks and crates from one of the freight cars. Farther down, I spy a few coach carriages. Their windows are fogged over, but I can make out the shapes of men inside, merchants in fur lined capes reading newspapers; a cassocked priest with his fingers steepled in front of him, praying or sleeping; soldiers playing dice and rolling cigarettes. None bother to look out of the windows. No one ever notices me.

A wave of dizziness passes through me when I look inside the last compartment. It is dimly lit, but I can tell there are two of them, a boy and a girl. Across from them sleeps a gaunt woman in drab dress. I stop my pacing and stare without blinking. The world in my periphery seems to stretch away from me, distances growing impossibly far so that there's only me and the sleeping figures. Then everything rushes back, like a stretched elastic band snapping back on itself, and I'm stepping forward, as if pulled by some invisible tether. I drop down lightly onto the wood planks, cross the platform, and slip aboard.

I know Pasha will be angry with me. He will say in that thin, sombre voice of his, *You promised.*

But I cannot stop.

I tell myself it's just one look. Nobody will know. Nobody will mind if I just watch them. I only want to watch the rise and fall of their chests as they sleep.

The boy leans his head against a rolled blanket. His hair haloes his face in dark whorls. His sister's face has the same rosy complexion, the same dimpled cheeks. Her chestnut tresses are bound up by a bronze comb, and her hands are buried inside a rabbit fur muff. Her lips - so red, so full of life - move ever so slightly, as if reciting some forgotten poem. Across from them the dour matron clutches a rosary in birdlike hands, her face scowling into her slowly rising chest, and I decide that she cannot be their mother. Her face is too stern, rigid even in sleep, her cheeks too angular: the face of some spinster governess. She lets out a long wheezing exhale and begins to snore. She won't awaken soon.

I should leave, should return to Pasha.

The girl shifts in her sleep, murmurs something, and my whole body trembles in pangs of anticipation. I know that I cannot resist her, cannot resist myself, and I'm inside the compartment, standing beside the Sleeper, so near, so very near. I want to run my fingers through her hair, to caress her unblemished skin, and I'm leaning close to her, even closer. And then, only then, do I whisper.

She inhales with a long, languid sighing, and I smell the powdered scent of the governess, the rich animal odour of sweat, of fur, of the leathern seats. Her eyes flutter open, and everything seems clearer, more vibrant, the way the world looks after surfacing from underwater. I can make out the grain in the wood panelling, the lustre of the brass fixtures, the chequered patterning of threads in her scarf, even the variegated strands of hair on the furs.

I whisper, *Come.*

The Sleeper rises. The furs fall about her, and she exits the compartment without a sound, leaving its door open behind her, as if the wind itself has spirited her away. The others sleep on.

We make our way down the narrow aisle of the train and out onto the near-empty platform. In the distance the station master limps alongside the cars, weaving slightly, making his way toward the engine. We trot across the platform unseen, past the ticket office and into the cobbled street still slick with snow. The Sleeper's cheeks glow pink as she looks with me at the shuttered shops. The curtained windows of the homes above spill gauzy light onto us. I don't see Pasha watching. Perhaps he won't disturb us while we walk. The train won't leave for another hour at least. I can always have her back before it leaves and brag to

Pasha that I can be good. That I don't need him to tell me what to do.

I whisper to the Sleeper to hurry now, and we make our way past the church and the deacon's home, past the cemetery and its rimed stones, past the joiner's house and its velvet curtains. A light snow has begun to fall. The flakes weave and cartwheel then disappear in the shadows between the buildings. Ahead of us, a bobbing lantern lights the flakes like fireflies, and a cowled figure approaches: an old babushka wearing a faded cloak over her skirts. She nears us and raises her lantern higher casting weird shadows across her face. Pinpricks of light dance in her pupils.

'Who? Who are you?' she asks, her voice quavering, her eyes wide in astonishment.

I whisper to the Sleeper to say the only thing I can think of. 'I'm Zoe,' she says, and the truth of her words startles me and turns the woman's face grey.

'Bohze moi!' the woman cries and holds her hand to her mouth. She staggers back a step, almost collapses onto the snowy curb. Her breath sputters forth in ragged gasps, and she nearly drops her lantern. I pull the Sleeper along with me. The silence of the street swallows the sobs of the old grandmother, and we melt into the shadows of the last few houses.

The cobbled street fades into a rutted track. Soon even that disappears beneath a blanket of snow. Our feet crunch deliciously over the frozen ground, and I want to run, to leap, to feel the rush of wind about me. We laugh, and the Sleeper's voice shimmers across the wooded landscape. The lights of the village are behind us now. Tall pines and firs spring up around us and shelter us from the wind. The snow isn't as deep among the trees, and our feet move quickly across the sloping downs. Soon we reach the rowan grove and pause amid the circle of trees.

I look up. The snow has stopped; a starry patch of sky peers at us through the branches. We walk in circles about the grove. A northerly wind runs its fingers through the Sleeper's hair, and she closes her eyes and smiles. Grass spikes poke through our footprints, young spring shoots, ensconced in ice like delicate crystals. I help the Sleeper unlace her boots and slip them off and her stockings too. A faint warmth seeps in through her feet as she splays her toes in the dry, powdery snow. She kicks her feet, sends a plume of white flying through the air. She laughs, we both laugh, and we dance, kicking our feet high and whirling around. The stars spin dizzyingly above.

Pasha's voice slices through my reverie. *What are you doing?* he says. He hovers on the far side of the grove between two of the largest trees. His eyes are shining needle-points of starlight. They're almost all I can see of him.

We take a step toward him. I tell the Sleeper we must be brave. 'We just want to play with her. To dance,' she says.

Take her back, he says. His voice is quieter now, barely a whisper, but even more cutting.

I know that he's right. I know I should return her. I know I will feel miserable if I don't. There's a wetness on our cheeks and I realize that she and I are crying.

You mustn't take her any farther, Pasha says.

A wind off the lake carries the sound of splintering ice, calling me, calling her. The Sleeper's breath quickens, and I know what I must do.

I'm sorry, we say and push past Pasha. He says nothing, just looks at us with those pale, sorrowful eyes, and then recedes into the shadows. We walk faster, passing beneath more trees, and into the tumbledown clearing that spills out to the icy shoreline. When I look back, Pasha is nowhere to be seen.

Ahead of us the hemlock awaits. We kneel beside the stump,

and the Sleeper reaches into the hollow and buries her hand into the nest of ribbons and buttons. The icy metal of the necklace slithers across her palm. We shiver at the touch of all the different textures: the silk ribbons, the corduroy buttons, the tracery of the locket. I help the Sleeper remove the bronze comb from her hair. Her tresses fall about her face, the strands tickling our cheeks. We hold the polished comb in front of us. In it we can see our reflection, our shining eyes glinting, almost glowing in the starlight. We place the comb on top of my collection, and I don't want to leave this place, this moment, but another sound of cracking ice draws us forward like a siren's cry, pulls our limbs, our body, our entire singular self toward the yawning expanse of ice.

We slide across the mirrored surface, and we're laughing, reeling, almost falling over. The Sleeper shrieks with delight. Her voice peals across the wastes and into the silent trees that line the shore. We run faster, slipping and skidding. Her skirt billows out around us. The clouds shift in the sky, unveiling a gibbous moon. We spread our arms and lean our head back skyward to bathe in its light. Beneath us, shadowy shapes of feeding fish flee before our feet. And we run. Faster, ever faster. A beckoning wind pulls us along, and I feel as if we're flying.

Ahead the ice darkens, turns an almost inky black, and our feet are splashing through a slush of ice-melt. We kick up a spray of pebbled, icy water with each stride. Fissures form across the thawing surface, and I know we're close. Three more steps and the Sleeper's foot breaks through the lake's frozen rind. The water grabs us, pulls us down insistently, invitingly, deep into the lake's embrace.

I finally feel alive again.

The world turns blue and silver. I see a flash of scales dart above us, toward the light. I whisper to the Sleeper, 'Go farther, farther still,' and she kicks her legs, and we descend. The moonlight fades about us, but I see even more clearly, my vision growing stronger with a warmth that radiates about us and from within us, a smouldering glow of heat that starts at our fingers and courses along our limbs. 'We're almost there.' I whisper to the Sleeper, 'Go faster,.' But she no longer hears me, and our limbs are slowing. The warmth has faded, consumed by nothingness, as we sink lower and lower until we reach the other Sleepers. Their hair flows like tendrils of seaweed; their tattered dresses are colourless in the stygian dark. They turn to stare at me, their faces so serene, so sad, so terribly alone and abandoned.

Mother Died Yesterday
Pascale Presumey

Mother died yesterday.

The ladies from Greggs saw her from the window and called the police. Face flat on the pavement, she was, one hand stuck in her coat pocket.

When I arrived the women were still gathered around her, the smell of moist, warm dough and bacon surrounding her dead body.

The medic asked if she had a history of heart problems.

No. She had no history.

Father married her at sixteen. She cooked his tea and cared for him until he died seven years ago. After his death she cooked her tea and cared for herself, for what it was worth. There was little to do, she always said. She ate like a sparrow and did not need anything. And there she was now: a broken bird splattered on the pavement. That's what I told the medic.

I asked him about her wedding rings. She had been wearing both since Father died, but yesterday, I noticed straight away, her hand was all bare against the concrete. He shrugged. He didn't know.

I eyed the Greggs ladies suspiciously, which sent them trotting back to their counter.

The funeral home is called Strong and Sons. It is a simple and unpretentious name. Father would have approved.

Mr Strong Senior asked me to fetch one of mother's favourite outfits, a pair of shoes and one significant object. The 'significant object' is to be placed in her hands, in the open casket.

In her wardrobe hang ten or twelve versions of what seems to me the same gravy brown dress. The shoes too are like a flock of twins.

I wander round the house to find a significant object. In the past thirty-seven years she has showed no pleasure or attachment to any particular item of jewellery, clothing or knick-knack. If there are memories attached to the few items scattered around the house, I don't know them. The house itself is not particularly cared for and dirtier than I remember.

As I come down the stairs, I notice that the plaque thanking Father for forty two years of service as a clerk to the Small Claims Department of the County Court has been taken down, leaving a faded square on the wallpaper, ghost-like. In the kitchen, two wedding rings have been left on top of the fridge. I apologise in my head to the Greggs ladies.

After much wandering I opt for a small crystal vase. I choose it because it is pretty.

The neighbour declares to be 'grief-stricken'. I do not know the name of the neighbour who only moved in three years ago. After violently shaking my hand and slapping my back he gesticulates wildly: 'Chin up!', 'Onwards and Upwards!' and insists I must put an ad in the local paper. An advertisement in the paper will cost me £104.14. On the website, when faced with writing the message, my mind goes blank. I cut and paste the ad below for the late Stan, which is the only one without spelling mistakes. I am then asked if I would like to include a picture next to the message. The pictures provided include the silhouette of a cat, a football, dog paw prints, a train and several flowers.

'No icon' it is. The very same day the ad comes out, phone calls start coming in. I have never spoken to so many strangers in my life. The funeral is charming. Father would have found the level of conversation and noise appropriate for such an occasion. Old people mainly, who knew her from the market, the library and Father's work place. They do not look like they enjoy each other's company and don't have much to say about Mother.

Sausage rolls and sprinkled doughnuts have been bought from Greggs as a form of apology, and they are a success with the old people, but I am afraid Mother's grey living room carpet is now covered with pink and neon green sprinkles.

No one asks about the vase.

The house is silent again. I am sitting in the middle of it, not knowing where to start. I guess it will all have to be sold.

The phone rings, it's the Halifax about her credit card. The Halifax? My mother? A credit card? I croak like a parrot. My voice is ridiculously high-pitched and foolish. 'It is not possible' I finally manage to say, 'Father would not have allowed credit'.

Yes, she had a credit card, I am told, no, only in her name, she took it out seven years ago and over the past seven years has acquired debts of £5632.90 . ' She's missed two payments. She's over the limit now.' the young girl says.

When I ask why a pensioner would be given a credit limit of over £5000, the young girl does not know what to answer and simply says: 'Anyway, she did, and there it is.' Yes, there it is. £5632.90.

I ask for a statement to see what the money was spent on and tell the girl I will call her soon. She doesn't want soon. She wants a date. So I say, off the top of my head: '23rd January. 12.35'. She seems satisfied and says she will put it on the computer. Mother, it appears, is also overdrawn on her current bank

account by another £2,493 . I have bought a large black notebook and on the first page I write 'Bank: £2,493'. And then the
credit card amount. I will use a red pen for amounts owed, a
blue for things to do, and a green for 'Other'.

Her bank statements show only trips to Morrisons and
Marks and Spencer and many cash withdrawals. The amounts
of the daily shopping trips are huge too. £142.13 at Morrisons. £208.56 at Marks. I dig through the bins to find receipts.
Nothing.

Under the sink there are forty seven plastic bags, neatly
folded. In some of the bags I find receipts. Morrisons: Scottish
organic smoked salmon, £8.99, Charbonnel Hot Chocolate, £7
a tin, pomegranate and blueberry cordial, £4 a bottle, sparkling
rosé, £7.98, clove and mandarin candle, £6 each.

The list goes on and on and I find none of the family favourite: cauliflower, pickles, ham hock on a sunday. The cheese is
not even cheddar.

'Sparkling Rosé,' I say out loud, 'Clove and Mandarin.' I feel
like I am speaking a foreign language.

I write all the numbers in the book. There suddenly seems to
be an awful lot of green entries.

The Marks and Spencer receipts are even more puzzling:
cashmere jumpers, angora gloves, a silk dressing gown. There
are no traces of any of those items in the bedroom.

The neighbour knocks on the door as if the house is on fire
and asks me what I am going to do with the furniture. I have no
idea. He knows just the man. Slips a business card in my hand
of the man he knows. ' He'll look after you.' he shouts, walking
away. 'Attic Dreams' the card reads. It has a drawing of a little
house with a cloud above the chimney.

The man from the antique shop comes round to the house.
He says, 'I am sorry to say your Mam's furniture is worthless.

Only brown wood.' He lifts a couple of knick-knacks, looks under a china shepherdess's dress and shrugs. Nothing of interest, he rules.

He will take the small green vase on the window sill, though. I look at the green vase like I have never seen it before. I have never seen it before. There have never been flowers in the house.

The man from Attic Dreams hands over three £1 coins, which I pile up neatly and place on the bookshelf. Behind the three coins is a photograph album.

When the man leaves, I move the coins to look at the album.

Here we are, Mother, Father and I passing through history, sometimes fatter, then thinner, then plump again and all becoming greyer. We always seem to be wearing coats and scarves. Mother smiles but never looks at the camera. Father and I look ahead but don't smile. The photographs seem to stop about the time I left home, twelve years ago. After that blank pages. For some reason, I keep turning the pages, going from blank to blank, imagining what the following photographs would have been, but my mind is also blank. Suddenly in the middle of a page is a train ticket.

I fish the green pen out of my pocket and write in the book, 'Return Ticket to London Euston. Tuesday 26th March 2002. Departure: 9.48am.'

The ticket has been used. I peel the sticky layer and lift the ticket. On the back of it she has written in her own tiny handwriting: '69 Dean Street'.

I write that in the book too.

A large woman comes from Oxfam to collect Mother's clothes. The brown dresses, the black shoes, the beige rain jacket and the puce wool coat. She piles the dresses and shoes into separate bin bags. ' How old was she then?' she asks, chewing on something.

I don't know. I don't know how old she was. I did not even look at the death certificate, just folded it back in the envelope and stuck it in the manilla folder I called 'Mother'.

She rummages through the pockets of the two coats, pulls out an old hankie, a rubber band and four more train tickets, which she just throws on the bed. After the fat woman has left the house, I sit on the bed. The train tickets are all to London.

69 Dean Street is in the middle of Soho. It has a black door and seems like a condemned building. The man in the newsagent underneath says it is only used for meetings in the evenings. What kind of meetings? He doesn't know. 'There's a weird guy who comes in every Tuesday with a pony tail, black cape.' he chuckles. I shiver.

The following Tuesday at 7pm, I am back in Dean Street. An older gentleman with a grey ponytail and a long black cape is in front of number 69. He's carrying a large black book, quite like mine, and is struggling with the lock.

I introduce myself and he lights up when hearing my mother's name. When I tell him the news, he seems genuinely saddened. 'She was such a gem,' he says. 'Come in.'

Mother it appears, was a cherished member of the Soho Writers Group. Colin is their chairman. She was their best dressed author, he says. And so passionate about literature. The words 'gem', 'cherished' and 'passionate' disturb me. Even 'author' and literature make me uncomfortable. I wish he would not be so dramatic.

'Why Soho?' I ask. 'Why not join a local Writers Group?'

Colin laughs. 'Soho is not the sleazy heartland it used to be but it still has that air about it. She just loved the underworld!' He shows me examples of her work. Stories of prostitutes, small time gangsters, mysterious gentlemen helping poor girls. The style is elegant, grand even, and at times... erotic.

The stories are typed and for a moment I doubt they could be Mother's but at the bottom of each page, her signature, in large twirling letters, written with a fountain pen. The date reads January 2010.

'She even had a few published in alternative literary magazines, you know.' He seems proud: 'alternative', 'literary'. My throat feels dry.

I ask Colin how long she has been coming. He checks in his big black book. She became a member on the 20th March 2009. She started coming to meetings the following Tuesday. They suspected something was amiss when she didn't turn up to the last two. She'd not missed one in seven years.

I write it in my black book: '20th March 2009'.

'How do you become a member?' Noticing my own black book, Colin smiles and asks me if I write too. No. I shake my head violently, which makes me giddy. 'Not writing, recording,' I say. 'I like recording.' He nods.

'You fill in an application form and send it to us.'

He's talking as if I want to join. 'Have you got my mother's application form?' I ask, sweating a little.

He goes to the back of the room and fetches a red ring-binder. Inside each transparent pocket is an application form. He finds my mother's, written with a fountain pen, signed on the day of my father's death.

I sit in the panelled room, and hold on to the red velvet curtains for a minute. Colin lights a long dark cigar. The dark wood and red velvet of the room, the smell of tobacco and Colin's aftershave, a tad musky, are twirling inside me, and I am afraid I will be sick. Father hated smells.

I look through the window to try to scrub the room out of

my head. It is dark out there and I imagine her walking under those yellow street lights every Tuesday.

How did she get back? I suddenly panic. At what time do the meetings end? 7 to 9, every Tuesday. I don't understand. Was there a train leaving that late? At what time did she get home?

Colin laughs. 'Oh no. She did not go back. She stayed at the Bloomsbury, round the corner. Room 218. Only the best for Heather,' he says. Only the best.

As soon as I say her name, the manager of the hotel smiles and asks if she is well. He is concerned, he says. He's left a couple of messages on her mobile phone but received no answer. She had a mobile phone.

I tell him that Mother is dead. He seems shocked.

'A charming lady,' he says, 'very elegant. Such excellent manners.' He fetches two large cream leather suitcases from the store room. 'You might want to have these now.' he says.

I sit in reception and rest one of the suitcases on the coffee table. The zip does not make any noise. As the case opens, a sweet smell of perfume rises up. Inside:

Two tweed suits.

Three buttery cashmere jumpers.

Two silk nightdresses.

A pair of pale green suede shoes.

Pearls and diamanté brooches.

A black satin purse containing cash.

Opera glasses.

A small bottle of a perfume called Insolence.

The feel of silk under my fingers, the shine of the jewellery, the softness of a jacket's fur collar make me feel nauseous. I close my eyes and think of Greggs, of egg and chips, bus passes and doilies and I cry for a very long time.

The hotel guests appear a bit unnerved by my crying in such a public place but the manager lets me. In the second suitcase there are more clothes, books too, mostly by foreign authors, a bundle of notebooks held together by a satin ribbon, a silver fountain pen in a black leather box.

After a while I am able to stand up. I leave the two suitcases with the manager, asking him to give the clothes to the staff. I have only kept the purse full of cash to pay back some of her debts, the notebooks and the silver pen .

In the train, on my journey back, I take the fountain pen out of its black leather box. I place it on my knees, under the table and I stare at it. Her pen. A fat silver pen encrusted with crystals, surely too big for her hand, so ridiculously ostentatious, a mockery of all we have been, all we have done, a disgrace really, that's the word. The pen that wrote such filth and dirt and words belching out of the mouths of people we would never have had in the house.

The pen feels just right for my hand. It nestles between my fingers, sturdy, confident, nudging me to give it a go. As we pass Rugby I pull out the black book from inside my bag and sit it right on the table, in full view of all. I open the black book. The last three filled in pages are entirely green. I turn to a fresh page. The lid of the pen comes off with an elegant click.

At the top of the page I write the first line of the story which I have been waiting to tell for so many years.

'Father Died Today...'

The Cloud Monster
Grace Haddon

I'm ten years old, and I can't blow out the candles on my birthday cake.

We're standing around our tiny kitchen table, which is draped with a plastic cloth too thin to disguise the black marks underneath. It's a Spider-Man cake, slightly squashed from its ride home in an Asda bag.

Ben beams up at me, just tall enough to rest his chin on the table. His school uniform is still muddied from football, his hands smeared with icing from too many party rings.

Mum shakes out the flaming match and sets it down with deliberate care, like it's a bird's egg she doesn't want to crush. Then her hands wrap around Ben's shoulders and they sing to me.

Their voices are too loud in the little kitchen. Mum's high voice sounds in danger of breaking, and Ben claps his hands as he chants every other word.

A blob of melted wax dribbles into Spider-Man's left eye.

I burrow my nail into the thin plastic tablecloth and stare at the quivering little flames.

But I can't blow them out.

I'm fifteen, and I'm wondering when she's going to stop talking.

She always sits in that squashy armchair, her hair scraped

back in a ponytail and her face always carefully neutral. Like a news presenter waiting to read out a tragedy.

My gaze drifts up to the paintings of trees hanging on the white walls. The room is also carefully neutral, with its muted colours and shiny wooden floor. Session three, and it's yet more guff about 'exploring your memory' and 'developing a coping strategy'.

I look down at the coloured crayons in my hand and wonder if sticking them up her nose would count as a coping strategy. I know what my nightmares look like; I have them nearly every night. So far I've refused to talk about them. Why the hell would I want to draw them?

'This is pointless.' I toss the notepad down. Like it's any of her business anyway. Some things are too big to fit on a piece of paper.

Her newsreader face doesn't change. It's like I didn't even interrupt her.

'Perhaps if you can get your thoughts down where you can see them, you may find they will have less control over you.' Then her eyes soften just a fraction. 'Monsters can only exist inside your head, Carla.'

I stand up, fist clenching around the crayons. They bend in the heat of my hand.

'I'm done.' The chair skitters along the floor as I kick it away and head for the door. She doesn't try to call me back.

Something blue flashes at the edge of my vision, just as I reach for the door handle. I glance back.

There's a large window along this wall, half-hidden by shiny green blinds. On the road below, a fire engine winds through the traffic, flashing, flashing for people to get out of the way. Sunlight gleams on the steel teeth of a ladder. Then the sirens start to wail.

Light, dark, smoke, ash. Alarms, hands. Howling.

I spin and hurl the crayons against the wall. My little finger catches the windowsill and something cracks. Pain throbbing along with the pulsing in my ears. The white wall is marred with red and orange.

My therapist finally looks disapproving.

'You don't know anything.' The words come out shaking, but venomous as they escape my gritted teeth. 'Anything,' I say, and I leave.

I don't go to session four.

I'm six years old, and there are clouds in my room.

They float by my window, curling faintly in the street lights. Something in the house is beeping like an alarm clock. Next door, baby Ben is crying. And downstairs, our dog is howling.

I get out of bed, ease the door open and creep past the other bedrooms before Mum gets up to look after Ben.

There are more clouds downstairs. They swirl around my legs as I walk. Tickly clouds that make me cough.

Dad shouts from upstairs.

The howling is coming from the kitchen. Charliedog is old and big, but he's not allowed to wander the house at night in case he knocks something over. I wonder if he's had a bad dream.

The clouds are even thicker in the hallway. They're coming from under the door.

Ben's crying gets louder and I can hear Mum and Dad moving about. Probably angry about the alarm clock that won't stop.

The door handle is hot. It sears my skin as I hold it and tears spring to my eyes, but I twist and pull and the door opens.

Black smoke pours out and fills the hallway, a great rolling wave that blinds and chokes me. The corner of a wall digs into my back as I stumble.

A ball of fire charges out of the kitchen. It has four black legs and wide, mad eyes. A tongue lolling from a foaming, panting mouth. Fur tipped with flickering streams of light. And the stench of burning.

I scream and fall as Charliedog runs past, the wall of smoke billowing out behind him. Blackness claws at my eyes and creeps down my throat. I can't find the kitchen door or the stairs. I can't call for Mum.

I lie down on the cool floor and struggle to take a breath that isn't gritty and sour. Then I fall asleep.

I am very young, and someone is holding me.

We're sat by the old gas fire in the living room. I like to stare into the flames and then close my warm eyelids to keep the heat in. It's dark outside. I couldn't sleep because I'm scared of the monsters I saw on TV. They looked like big lizards and blew smoke from their noses. I'm scared that they'll take me away.

Dad tells me that monsters aren't real and they can't hurt me. I don't believe him, but I snuggle into his warmth and fall asleep to the rumble of his voice.

I'm six years old again, and someone picks me up.

Scratchy wool on my cheek, a rasp in my ear. I bury my face in Dad's jumper and try to breathe in his scent, but all I smell is burning. I'm so dizzy that I can't lift my head. Charliedog isn't howling any more.

'It'll be all right Carla,' he says in my ear. 'I promise. You're going to be fine.'

I don't believe him. I'm sure that the clouds are going to get us. But I cling on and close my eyes as he carries me through the house. I can't stop coughing, but when I do I just breathe in more clouds.

He's coughing too, big shuddering coughs that make me scared he'll drop me. Coughs that shake me enough to make my teeth rattle. Mum always tells him he needs to take it easy because the doctor said he has weak lungs.

I don't want Dad to die.

So I cling to him and cough, my eyes squeezed shut against the hot clouds that get hotter. I don't know where Mum and Ben are. I don't know where I am.

Everything is shaking and spinning. With nothing left to ground me, I lose my grip and fall.

Dad's jumper becomes a slippery plastic coat. His breaths are slow and wheezy, the hands gripping me are gloved and hard. When I look up, his face is made of shiny smoke and there are metal bits where his mouth is.

I fight against the cloud monster.

He runs with me, out of the smoke, and then there is darkness and cold air and the shouting of sirens. Neighbours gather nearby, their faces scared and angry and sad.

Mum is standing on the pavement, clutching baby Ben and shivering in her pyjamas. She crouches down and hugs me so tightly that I feel giddy again.

I look back at the man who isn't Dad. He's turned away from us, shaking his head as he watches our house burning down. There are others with him, too. None are moving. I can't see Charliedog.

Eyes streaming from the smoke, I look at each and every face around us. Family, friends, strangers.

I can't see Dad.

I finally take a breath and scream.

I'm ten years old, and I can't blow out the candles on my birthday cake.

I scrunch up my face until my eyes are slits, turning the flames into wobbly white lights. The dreams haven't left me, of Dad and Charliedog and the cloud monster, and to this day I've never spoken of what happened. The memories will stay with me forever.

Mum's voice quavers as the song draws to a close.

Ben pokes me in the side. 'You have to make a wish first,' he whispers.

I breathe in, and the smell of burning wax clogs my throat. There's ringing in my ears: the wail of sirens. Everything feels distant. For a moment the fireman is reaching for me, gloved hand stretching across the flames.

I breathe out through pursed lips, blowing out the candles one by one. I keep pushing the air from my lungs until it feels like I'm suffocating, but I can't stop. Not until the last, lonely candle has gone dark and there is only blackened wax and wafts of smoke and Mum's white fingers as she squeezes Ben's shoulders.

I wish that monsters weren't real.

Masquerade Night
Alex Shvartsman

The first time Harat saw Ada was when she was dancing with the goddess of death.

It was masquerade night, and Club Rhythm was full of monsters. An orchestra blasted the latest European tunes at their highest volume setting, filling the cavernous dance hall with music. Dance beats reverberated in Harat's temples. An engine rotated an enormous lantern of painted glass suspended from the high ceiling, which cast shards of coloured light across the hall. It was the glint of light against the lapis-lazuli amulet that drew his attention.

The amulet reminded him of the jewellery once worn by the women of his tribe, but the smoke and glitter of the club swallowed up the details of the trinket, much like the depths of time had long swallowed all memory of his tribe's existence, leaving him alone, an abandoned godling devoid of followers. It was a fate shared by most of the celestials who frequented Club Rhythm.

Once upon a time, creatures like him had ruled the world, lording it over the terrified humans. But the world had changed, the humans had multiplied, had unlocked the secrets of bronze and iron and steam. They took over, and their one-time gods, stripped of much of their power, were now confined to the shadows.

By 1920s, they could mingle with humans freely only on rare occasions. All Hallows Eve, Purim, Mardi Gras - the holidays of masks, when gods and spirits could work the streets of New York City in their true form without anyone giving them so much as a second look. Then Jumis bought the nightclub and came up with the weekly masquerade night - costumes required - a place and time where someone like Harat wouldn't stand out despite his feline eyes and pointy ears.

Harat tapped into his Leopard aspect, using the cat vision to study the amulet from across the hall, noting the subtle differences in the design. It was not a lost artefact of his people, merely an inexpensive trinket. He felt a pang of disappointment, but then his gaze travelled upward and zeroed in on the face of the woman who wore it. She was stunning.

Her face was flushed as she danced not so much with the goddess of death as around her. Enthralled by the celestial's power she circled ever closer, almost touching her and then shrinking back, like a moth fluttering around a light bulb. The little moth would eventually get too close, and her life would be extinguished, all too soon.

Normally, Harat would not interfere. He didn't prey upon humans, but for many of the other gods the club was hunting grounds. It wasn't his business to impede the natural order of things. But this time - this one time - he was compelled to act.

Harat strode across the dance floor, pushing past the writhing bodies, human and celestial, until he was face to face with his target. Miru, the Polynesian goddess of the underworld, was tall and very thin, and her skin was of reddish hue. She could have almost passed for a severely sunburned human were it not for her shark teeth - several rows of sharp, jagged white daggers.

Harat stopped right in front of the goddess, inserting himself into the enthralled woman's orbit. The tall celestial scowled at him and Harat threw the contents of the glass he was holding into Miru's face. Before the other celestial could react, Harat turned around and headed toward the coat room. The confrontation was coming, and it wouldn't do for the humans to witness it. Miru roared in frustration and pursued Harat, taking on her Shark aspect as she moved. The enthralled woman stopped dancing, and was blinking rapidly, like someone who had been suddenly awakened from deep sleep.

When Miru burst into the coat room, empty for the summer, Harat was ready for her. The Leopard aspect took over and he jumped his opponent in a blur of claws and fangs. The two primal forces clashed, Shark against Leopard, tearing into each other, cutting and slashing, and moving faster than a human eye could follow. The thumping dance beat concealed the sounds of their struggle.

When it was over, Harat limped outside. He was bleeding from several long gashes on the side of his torso just below the shoulder, but could still move under his own power. What was left of the Shark covered the floor, the walls, and some of the ceiling of the coat room.

Harat searched the club, but the woman wearing the lapis lazuli amulet was gone.

'What were you thinking?' Jumis, the Latvian god of the harvest, stared Harat down. 'I've got a good thing going here. I don't need you muddying up the waters.'

'It won't happen again,' said Harat. His bandaged ribs ached pleasantly, reminding him of the battles past.

'It better not,' said Jumis. 'Do you have any idea how much the repairs are going to cost me?'

Harat was envious of the other celestial. Pudgy and greying at the temples, Jumis looked human, ordinary enough to intermingle with mortals without having to pretend he was wearing costume and makeup for a masquerade ball. For that alone, Harat would trade places with this lesser god, if he only could.

'You still owe me, from when I aided you in Constantinople,' said Harat.

'They call it Istanbul now, and not any more I don't,' said Jumis. 'You better believe this little temper tantrum of yours makes us even. Next time you feel like a fight to the death, perhaps when your sparring partner's friends decide to avenge her, you take it outside.'

Harat leaned against the wall. 'No one is coming to avenge her,' he said. 'Relics like us have no friends.'

Harat tried to forget the incident. He had lived for too long and fought too many battles to remember the details of each kill. But, every time he closed his eyes and tried to sleep, he saw the enthralled woman's face, her eyes as blue as the amulet she wore.

He'd been with human women many times in the past. He sought some kind of connection, a balm to soothe the pain and anguish, the grief he still felt over the loss of the mortals of his tribe. None of those other women made him feel the way he did when thinking about her.

Harat came to the club on the next masquerade night, and the one after that, but there was no sign of the woman. She must have been scared off by the experience, some deeper part of her mind subconsciously recognizing the peril even if she had never learned first-hand how dangerous her dance with the Shark should have been.

Having existed for thousands of years, Harat knew patience. He came to the club every week and roamed the hall, a glass of absinthe in hand, watching the humans who were dressed like monsters, and the monsters pretending to be human.

His persistence had paid off. He finally saw her, not on the dance floor this time, but sharing a small round table with Qarib, the Persian god of serpents and poison.

'She sure knows how to pick the winners,' thought Harat.

He approached the table and hovered over the diminutive form of the Persian poison god.

'Leave,' he told the Snake.

The smaller celestial hissed at him, but didn't wish to fight. The word of what happened to the Shark had spread quickly among the club regulars. He scooted from the table without saying a word. Harat pulled the chair back and took the seat across from the woman. For several moments, they contemplated each other.

'That wasn't very nice of you,' said the woman.

'He isn't a very nice fellow,' said Harat.

She pouted. 'Maybe so, but he was going to buy me a drink.'

'You wouldn't enjoy drinking anything he might have offered you. Regardless, that is an easy fix. I'll buy you a drink instead. My name is Harat.'

'Ada,' said the woman. She continued to study him with those big, blue eyes. 'And are you a nice fellow, Harat?'

'By the standards of this place? I should say so,' said Harat.

She smiled at him. 'In that case, I will have to consider letting you buy me that drink, sometime.' Then she picked up her purse and walked away, without turning to look back even once.

The Leopard god wanted very much to pursue her, but centuries of experience had taught him both patience and the wisdom of knowing when not to push his luck.

It was many months later that he saw Ada again. She wore a flowing green dress and covered her face with a hand held Venetian half mask, but Harat knew her scent now and could find her in a crowded club, regardless of whatever disguise a human was capable of using.

He approached just as Silenus, a satyr with a taste for human flesh, was trying out his pick up line on her. Harat inserted himself unceremoniously between the two of them at the packed bar counter.

'Hello, Ada,' he said. 'You've had a long time to think about that drink. Have you reached a decision?'

'You're very persistent,' she said, and she nodded towards her cocktail glass. Harat motioned for the bartender to mix another. 'And also very consistent. You're wearing the same costume again?'

'It suits my nature,' Harat brushed at his whiskers. 'I like leopards.'

'I'm more of a dog person,' said Ada, but she didn't refuse the drink, or another after that.

The evening wore on as they spoke about architecture and dead poets, straining their vocal chords to be heard over the music. For the first time in his very long existence, Harat was beginning to fall in love.

She asked him to walk her home, and he almost refused. He cared about her, and he was afraid of what would happen if he went with her now, and she found out that the whiskers and the fur didn't come off. He never really fretted about that moment of truth with any of the other women - some denied him, some were excited by what he was - but Ada was different. So he nearly refused to go with her, but then he saw her moving unsteadily on her feet and thought back to the Shark, and the Snake, and the Satyr, and dozens of other predators that surrounded them, and he had no choice at all.

He offered his arm and the two of them left the club together. They walked the midnight streets and their two shadows, cast long in the dim glow of the street lights, merged into one.

The walk was over all too soon. It turned out that she lived only a few blocks away from the club and she invited him to come upstairs. He looked into her big, blue eyes and, despite his concerns about losing her when she learned the truth, he followed her inside.

They came up the stairs of the town-house and into her home, and she poured him a glass of red wine. They sat on the couch in her living room and they talked some more, until the world began to swim in front of Harat's eyes. He tried to get up but he lost his balance and tumbled onto the thick rug, the wine glass rolling out of his hand and leaving a trickle of wine that looked like blood drops in its wake.

Harat tried to shift into his Leopard aspect, but he could not. He couldn't move at all, his ageless body betraying him utterly. All he could do was to move his eyes, following Ada as she stood above him, frowning.

'Why?' he tried to ask, but all that came out were some guttural sounds.

'Poor kitty-cat,' she said. 'You should have known your place. You should have stayed away from me.' She walked out of his field of vision, but her velvety voice continued on from elsewhere in the apartment. 'You weren't my intended prey. I only hunt the really bad ones, the murderers, the monsters.'

He concentrated on her voice, zeroed in on it to stay awake, stay focused, and he reached deeper and deeper within himself searching for the Leopard but finding only the abyss, its darkness inching ever closer, enveloping his mind.

'You were too persistent for your own good, kitty-cat, scaring away the game.' She returned and bent over him, still wearing the flowing green dress with the blue lapis lazuli amulet gleaming against the silk. She was holding a large carving knife. 'So, you forced my hand. Nothing personal, but a girl's got to eat.' She shrugged and smiled at him one last time, and plunged the knife deep into his chest.

As the cold steel bit deep, his consciousness reached desperately into the furthest corners of the abyss and found the Leopard aspect. His body transformed around the blade stuck hilt-deep in his midsection. The Leopard twisted, swatting at Ada, and his claws connected, leaving three deep gashes on the side of her neck and her shoulder.

Ada gasped in surprise and stumbled back, letting go of the knife. The great cat pounced, pinning her down on the carpet, his fangs and claws ripping into her, causing as much damage as possible before the knife wound sapped his strength.

She pushed him off with surprising strength, throwing him towards the couch. His feline body twisted and he swiped at her one more time. She moved away with impossible speed, but the claw snagged at the string that held the amulet, and ripped it from her neck.

The blue stone set in silver flew across the room and hit the wall with a clatter. As soon as it left Ada's neck, her body transformed. It changed almost instantly, the visage of a woman replaced by a thing made of teeth and tentacles, an ancient horror from long before the first humans created the first gods by worshipping the fire and the stars and the predators around them.

Harat faced the nightmarish creature and roared in pain and anger. The thing that used to be Ada roared back, and her war cry sounded like a mix of distant thunder and crumbling gravestones. The two beings, forgotten by history, came at each other.

Harat woke up naked, lying in the pool of blood and grime and ripped tentacles. The sun was beginning to set outside - it had been at least a day since the fight. His fingers brushed against the crusted blood and scabbing skin, where the knife wound used to be. The wound hadn't fully healed yet, but it would in another day or so. He wasn't much of a god any more, but he could still heal much faster than mortal men. He would survive.

He got onto his feet and limped across what was left of Ada's living room. He found the bathroom and climbed into the cast iron tub, turning on the shower and letting the room-temperature water cleanse his body. He caught some water in his mouth, trying to wash out the taste of the ancient god's blood. He ran the shower until the container suspended above the tub ran out of water.

He emerged from the bathroom and stepped carefully around the worst of the mess in the living room until he reached the other side and picked up the lapis lazuli amulet. He turned to the shard of a mirror that remained on one of the walls and put the amulet on, the silver setting cold against his skin.

He watched his reflection as his cat irises expanded and rounded out, his fur disappeared, revealing smooth skin, and his ears lost their sharp feline tips. Soon he was looking at the reflection of an average young man. Even his Leopard nose sensed only a human.

Harat rifled through the apartment's closets until he found some clothes that would fit him, left over no doubt, from one of Ada's previous victims. He got dressed, left the apartment, and walked downstairs.

Although the sun was setting, it was still daylight. He watched from the doorway as throngs of people walked past the town house, cars and horse-drawn carriages competed for road space, and street vendors called out to the passers by, advertising their wares. It was the world devoid of masks and camouflage, a new world that he hadn't been privy to, that left him and his kind behind, masquerading in the shadows. A world meant for humans.

He took a deep breath, opened the door, and stepped outside, joining them in the light.

The Woman Next Door
Tracy Fahey

I'm tired all the time since he came. Tired and overwhelmed and overpowered by the feelings, the smells, the sounds, the weight and feel of him. He was part of my body, sleeping tight under my skin. Now he's out, we're apart yet never-apart, all at once. His warm, soft scent, the silken fluff of his head, the tiny perfection of his feet, all these fill my senses; they intoxicate me. I love him. I resent him. He's the biggest thing that's ever happened to me. He's everything, all the time. My body is still connected to his through a complex and invisible set of nerve endings. His cat-cries wake me, alert, when I doze. Sometimes I see Sean, a lump of sleep beside me, and my foggy brain thinks it might hate him if I ever had the time or energy to do so,

It's only been three weeks and my home has been invaded. Its new, tiny overlord has possessions strewn everywhere. Clothes horses are filled with drying babygros, there are a pile of presents at the foot of the stairs that I'll take up someday when I remember. It's horrifying. In the minutes here and there, when I come out of my baby-haze of sleepwalking through life in odd socks, I see my home, layered in dust, piles of laundry in the kitchen and smeared surfaces everywhere. Part of me knows this is just a phase, but the rest of me is just quietly appalled by my own descent. Sometimes I catch sight of my face flashing up in a mirror, a glass pane, startled, pale, haunted, and I wonder, 'Is this me?' Can this really be the me I remember from a scant few months ago, that woman in heels, hair pulled back smartly in a shining chignon, Kate Spade handbag in one hand, mobile phone in the other? I can see her, as if through a mist, but I no longer believe I was her. My hair is always knotted now; it's been in the same ragged ponytail for days. Yesterday I dropped my mobile in the baby bath, and my glossy handbag has been replaced by a pouchy, plastic hammock from M&S, stuffed with nappies and bottles. My body hurts, stiff and sore, so I swathe it carefully in layers of soft, brushed cotton, worn track pants, fluffy bed socks, anything that's large and comforting to wear. My belly still juts out, embarrassingly so, as if he's still in there. I love him, but this is what he's done to me. He has taken me over.

The woman next door isn't like that. I can't stop watching her. She's our new neighbour, moved in when I was in hospital. She is everything that I want to be. As I sit up at night, rocking him to sleep; that ancient, ageing ritual of soothing a mewling child, I see her come home, her heels tap-tapping smartly on the pavement, her long blonde hair swaying behind her, glinting under the street lights. She's glossy and pretty in a carefully manicured way - I bet she has a great manicure too. Her clothes are a symphony of creams and caramels, swingy camel capes, belted French trench coats, tissue soft brown leather jackets. I imagine their smell, warm and fragrant like a subtle floral perfume. Her figure is elegant; she strides confidently about in knee-high boots, her slender thighs inspiring a soft, sad kind of lust in me. On the days when the baby cries unstoppably, when the noise fills my head till I think I might scream too, I want to be her so badly, I half-wonder if I can simply will it to happen.

Sean can't understand my fascination with her.

'She's only a woman, for God's sake,' he says dismissively. We are having a miserable meal, microwaved rice and chicken in a sauce from a jar. It says 'Tikka Masala' on the label, but it's rust-brown and smells faintly of gas. I just know that next door, the woman is laying down heavy, silver cutlery on dense, white napkins, lighting candles, and bringing food carefully out of the oven, a herbed omelette perhaps, or a perfect chocolate soufflé. I push away my plate of lukewarm rice mush. Sean is eating away steadily, his hair rumpled from his long commute home on the train. He looks tired too, but I have no pity. He goes away every weekday to a place with coffee that other people make. He talks to grown-ups for pleasure, about the weather, TV, sports. People invite him for lunch… A thin, seagull cry blurts from the baby monitor. I'm already on my feet, moving instinctively upstairs. My legs are leaden, like when you get out of water after swimming. When I get to the cot, he's back asleep, his fat little body gloriously splayed, his face twisted in a majestic, thunderous frown. I love him. I hate him.

I sit beside him and look out the window into the neighbouring backyard. A soft pool of light gleams, illuminating her neatly cut grass, her trimmed hedges. She's sitting out there, on one of her cast iron chairs, her legs neatly crossed, a glass in front of her and a book. I feel my insides twist with envy. I remember all those days I sat carelessly half-reading, flicking through pages, those marvellously blank, indolent days of pregnancy; how I took that idleness for granted. Now I'm a perpetual-motion mummy-machine, picking up, wiping, soothing and feeding. I touch my fingers to the pane, lightly. She tilts her head to one side and looks directly up at me. I jump back from the window as if it has shocked me, ashamed, embarrassed to be caught staring like an envious wraith from a darkened window.

'Laura!' It's Sean, I remember. These days I forget him as soon as he leaves the room, I run down the stairs silently, angrily.

'Don't shout!' I hiss. 'Don't wake him.'

Sean looks abashed. 'Sorry,' he says contritely. 'Can I go up and see Jack?' I sit down. It's still strange to me that he has a name. In my head he is just Him, all powerful, almighty Him.

'Sure,' I say listlessly. 'But don't wake him. I need some time. I need to do...' I wave a limp hand at the congealed dishes, the dirty table, the spattered wads of kitchen roll, '...this.' He nods and disappears upstairs. I pick up the plates and put them in the sink, then just stand there, dull and unmoving, hands on the sticky draining board. He's too much. It's too much. I can't do it. No one told me it would be so incessant. I am not me any more. I am a corpulent mummy-monster, performing endless placatory rituals to assuage a screaming, soaking god. I sigh, a deep, juddering sigh, and then hunker down and open the fridge to start preparing bottles for the night feeds. I hear the monitor crackle, then there's a hiccup, a choke and a wail. I close my eyes, feeling the light of the refrigerator dance pink behind my eyelids. I put the bottles back, as delicately as the anger in me will allow.

It's morning. I watch her from the kitchen window. She comes out in that smart cape with the three sparkling buttons at the neck, leather satchel over one shoulder, carrying a pink baby seat. Yes. I haven't told you about that. It's the worst bit. She has a baby too. She has a baby and she looks terrific. Her body is slim and elegant, her clothes are carefully chosen and co-ordinated. Her baby girl never seems to scream. I can see her face quarter-turned away as she gently places the baby seat in the back of the car. Every day she drops her off and goes to work, that magic place where no one soils themselves, or spits up milk, or cries for hours, endlessly, mysteriously. She is everything I am not. Quick, she's seen me. She turns on one heel and waves at me brightly, before stepping in to her car. I stand there, lumpish, tired, my hair itching with grease, my skin grey and dry as sandpaper and I cry fat, silent, oozing tears. I feel full of sadness, swollen with misery, as if the slightest bend or tilt might unleash a wave of tears from over the barricades of my eyelids.

I don't even know her name. I pretend it is something exotic: Anais, Veronique, Isolda. In my imagination she runs a magazine or a model agency. She drinks skinny cappuccinos and goes shopping for shoes at lunchtime.

Sean is getting increasingly annoyed by my obsession. 'How much time do you spend mooning over her? Couldn't you just introduce yourself?'

I can't explain why not, why her very presence fills me with shame for my weakness, my bulk, my secret tears.

'I'm sure she's grand,' he continues. 'I sometimes see her on the train and she looks friendly. She's said hello once or twice. Go on, why don't you make friends? Her baby would be company for Jack when he's older. Besides, she's probably lonely.'

I don't think she's lonely, even though I've never seen anyone else visit the house. I think she's self-contained, precise and perfect in her pristine glass bubble of a life. Sean has no idea what she means to me. I look at him eating tonight's culinary disaster - pork chops and potato, no vegetables and no sauce - and feel a gush of hot hatred for his solid, chewing head.

Days go by. I wish I could say I get used to it all. But I don't. Instead I stumble in a grey fog, vision blurred with tiredness but guided by a series of bat-squeaks and howls, as I try to calculate what's needed, what's happening, what's hurting. Sometimes when I arrive at the cot his eyes squint crossly at me, like a middle manager of a supermarket upbraiding the checkout staff. I want to cry and apologise. Once I fell asleep hanging over his cot; when I woke up he was staring at me, affronted, face contorted in a dreadful infant rage.

Somehow I blunder through it, the dull days of crying and laundry, the nights of pacing and rocking. Sean is out there somewhere in the ether, a shadowy presence, whose life intersects with mine in the evenings. We've established a new mode of being; a badly-cooked meal in return for stories from the outside world. We're slipping away from each other, fast and silent, as the days go by. I remember being in love with him, but distantly. It seems like a poor, weak thing compared to this compulsive baby-need that surrounds me. We're more of a team now, me chief nurse, him a disinterested supervisor. But I try. I cook quick, hopeless meals: beans on toast, pasta and ready-made tomato sauce, canned chili. And he talks about Veda.

See? I was right. Her name was exotic. He's struck up a few chats with her and every evening I question him like a detective. She is, he thinks, in her mid-thirties. She doesn't seem to have a boyfriend. She runs a travel agency, so instead of picturing her flicking frosty glances over starved model bodies, I visualise her spinning a globe with one painted fingernail as she talks to a client. She has a baby girl. He thinks she is called Kate or Katie. I feel a stab of envy that she can choose to discuss her child or not, that she neatly divorces woman from mother every morning when she steps on that train. Sean asks me if we should invite her over. I demur. He shrugs. I don't tell him my pathetic fantasy of looking better and losing weight before we meet. This fantasy gets more hopeless by the day, as I stand over the sink eating buttered toast with jam in fast, shameful, secret bites.

One day I do bump into her. He's been crying all day so I manhandle him into the pram, the stiff starfish shape of him rigid in protest, and strap him in.

'We'll see if being outside helps,' I tell him desperately. I trundle the pram across the gravelled drive which bumps him and makes him crosser. At the gate I pause to open it when, oh no! It's her! At her gate! I can't escape.

'Hello, 'I say miserably. I drop my gaze and see myself with a shock of revulsion, a stained tracksuit, a pair of Sean's socks, dirty Crocs.

'Hello there,' she whispers back. She's carrying her perfect daughter in a neat baby sling. She puts a finger to her lips. 'Sleeping,' she breathes, and I nod, relieved to have an excuse not to talk. From the pram comes a low, choking wail. I look at him, sticky face, open, gummy mouth and feel an absurd desire to grab her sleeping child and run off, leaving my yowling one behind. Of course I don't. I smile, bob my head quickly in a meaningless gesture, and push the pram through the gate.

'So you finally met Veda?' asks Sean that evening, settling down his worn leather man bag. I should get him a new one I think, and then automatically add it to the never-ending list of things to get, like underwear that fits me, cleaning spray, a new lawn mower. 'She was delighted to finally meet you; she even said she might call over. I told her this evening would be fine.' He looks at me expectantly.

I am startled. 'What? I can't do this evening. It's my new fitness class!' He looks blank, as well he might. I've just made it up, but am banking on his bad memory.

'But it would be nice for you,' he coaxes. I look around wildly at the chaos; our life, me, and I know I can't have it examined by the perfect woman next door.

I have to leave for my imaginary class, so I drive around aimlessly until I see a coffee shop open. I order a sweet, rich mocha and sip it till the heat and the sugar warms me up. For an hour, a whole glorious hour, I watch people go by, chat, drink coffee. I read a newspaper someone's left behind and eat a cranberry oat cookie. It's heavenly. For the first time in almost two months I feel myself relax, feel that I can do this strange and complex thing called motherhood. I just need a break; to remember that the world of restaurants, hotels and magazines still exists out there.

When I come home the house is peaceful. Sean is watching TV, the dishwasher is thrumming away gently and the landfill of clutter seems to have receded. I sling my gym bag over the chair and breathe in deeply.

'Is he...?'

'Asleep,' confirms Sean. 'Pity you missed Veda. She got a babysitter in and everything. And she was great with Jack. She had him off in minutes, sang to him. She even gave me a hand with the tidying.'

My stomach sinks; there's a red knot of shame in my throat.

'Oh,' I say, faintly. Sean gets up and hugs me.

'And it's so good for you to get out more. Veda says it's important.' I lie into his hug, trying to forget the embarrassment of another woman cleaning up my filthy home. He kisses my hair, beside my ear.

'Tell you what,' he says thickly, into my hair. 'Tomorrow's Saturday. Take a few hours off in the morning. Treat yourself.'

And I do. The next morning I leave without the heavy buggy or the car-seat. A miracle of unimpeded motion. I go to a big, cheap high street store and buy some smart ankle boots, a long, soft cardigan, a cheap but colourful necklace, and a forgiving, pretty smocked top. I go into the public toilets and change out of my old tracksuit and trainers and stuff them in a bin. I'll probably regret this when I get home, but I can't bear to keep them now. I have my hair cut and blow dried. I don't care that the junior washing my hair is appalled by its state.

'It's awful tangled,' she says dubiously. 'I'll have to cut it up a bit.' When I come home, hair bobbed neatly and smelling of some mysterious, fruity product, I feel transformed.

'Look at you!' Sean's approval shines out at me. He takes my arm and rotates me, carefully, as if he held me too hard, this shiny new vision might crack and unleash my old tattered self.

'Thank you.' I say softly. 'Thank you for remembering me.' He smiles, that old, warm smile that always makes my mouth curl upwards in response.

'That's not all,' he says. 'Look!'

I see two suitcases in the hall. Is he going? Am I? I turn, momentarily terrified.

'It's a treat,' he says, half-laughing at my surprise. 'We're off to that nice B&B we went to for Claire's wedding. Just us.'

My heart is beating blood through my ears in a long, drowning roar.

'Where is he?'

'Jack's fine,' says Sean confidently. 'Veda has him. She offered. We've been planning this for you for a while. I knew you needed a break.' He pauses and smiles at me. 'She just helped me with the final details.'

I am weak, dizzy. 'You gave him to her?' My voice is coming from somewhere outside me, weak and breathy. Everything inside me is focusing on staying upright.

'Yeah. He's over there right now…Wait! Are you OK?' His voice is alarmed. I look at him and start running. I pelt down the garden path, one of my stupid new boots I was so proud of buckles under me and throws me to the ground. I land, palms flat on the gravel that bites into my flesh like knives. I register the pain somewhere at the back of my mind, but I keep running, then I'm there, pounding on her door.

'Where is he?' I shout. Sean is behind me, grabbing my wrists.

'Shhh!' he says hoarsely. 'Stop it!' A woman on the road has paused to watch, two children have stopped cycling to stare instead. I don't care.

'Let me in!' I'm ringing the doorbell frantically between repeated knocks. There's no answer. Sean is calling my name, urgently, over and over. I can't look at him. 'I was in the hairdressers!' I think wildly. 'I was buying clothes!' Instantly I need him, I need his warm heft in my arms, his milky breath against my neck. My baby; the most solid, true and beautiful miracle of my life. I've started crying now, deep, grating sobs. No-one's answering the door. I'm beyond caring what I do. I pick up a smooth, spherical stone from her rockery and lob it through the thick glass pane on the front door. My hand scrapes through and opens the snib lock. It comes out red and wet. Sean tries to grab it.

'Jesus! What've you done!' But I'm off, inside, running.

'Where are you?' I run, crying, heels clattering through an immaculate kitchen, then a bare sitting room. I'm terrified - cold, stone terrified. I run upstairs, tripping as I go, then into a bedroom. It's show home neat. Nothing. Nobody.

'Laura,' calls Sean. He stands in the doorway of her bedroom. 'She must be here. Her baby's still in the cot.' His face is stunned with relief.

There's a pink, ruffled cot by the window. I whirl around and stand over it. My vision comes and goes in one big, sick blur. I open my mouth, but only a wet, animal sound comes out. In that one, awful moment, I realise it all, the perfection of her home, her limpid, graceful lifestyle. I think wildly of my baby, of his soft starfish fingers pulsing towards me, his hiccuping cry, the warm weight of him on my lap. I open my mouth and finally I name all those things, those smells, sounds, sights, my feelings. 'Jack,' I say softly.

But it's not Jack. What looks back at me, waxen and lifeless, is a doll.

Red Feet
Siobhan Logan

Dancing was her one addiction. An interlude of abandonment in this careful life. The bar's air-conditioning ruffled her crocheted top, goose-bumping her exposed skin. The black top and matching mini-skirt were charity-shop finds but she'd splashed out on maroon leopard-print tights. As Jess made for the dance-floor, her stride lengthened like a panther on the prowl.

With a loosening shrug of her shoulders, she watched her black pixie-boots tapping out the beat. Find the rhythm. Move with it, ride it. Feet first, her body following like a bystander caught in the mêlée.

'For all the broken-hearted out there,' the DJ boomed, as he switched to the reggae beat of *Love is an Addiction*. The Students Union was adorned with red plastic hearts with STOP signs: slogans read 'Cupid is Stupid' or 'Love Bites'. Jess laughed, punching one of the disco mobiles playfully. And now her movements were molten, spilling out of the rhythm while the leopard-skin spots winked like jungle eyes.

At the segue a musical phrase stole over her. It was the rap cover of *Killing Me Softly*, her mother's favourite. They used to giggle together, practising their sexy moves to it in the living room, when there was just the two of them. Jess was too young to understand the yearning in her mother's body. But grasping it now, she slithered into the music's embrace, sliding her hips as if rubbing against a lover, joy and melancholy rippling out to her fingertips.

'I got you Babe,' a male voice growled in her ear. She flinched away from the body pushing in behind her.

'Don't stop now,' he crooned.

Without missing a beat, her flailing arms struck out, her feet fiercely stamping the drum tattoo. Her dancing spirit was a demon not to be messed with. She didn't relent until he disappeared back into the throng. But he'd spoiled the mood. Now her mother's song only stirred up a familiar cocktail of grief and guilt. When the music switched to a bubble-gum girl-band number, Jess retreated.

The Student Union bar was filling up. For an Anti-Valentine's Day party, there was some obvious snogging in the booths from singletons who'd scored. Or maybe they'd been faking indifference all along. For a moment, she pictured Sam beside her. They'd have laughed together at the mock bravado of the slaughtered Cupid posters. Before he squeezed into her regulation single bed in the student house. Shaking her head, she punctured that thought-balloon.

In the distance she spotted her house-mate's group. Chloe was cupping a hand to somebody's ear, her Rapunzel hair falling loose. The party'd been Chloe's idea. Determined to stave off Valentine's blues after her first-term break-up, she'd rounded up film course friends, all male. With Chloe's female buddies out on dates or departed for Reading Week, Jess was the stand-in. An interloper from Business School. The men were busy on their phones. She mustered a friendly-neutral tone, her default-setting.

'Oh cheers,' she said, reclaiming her stool. The cocktails were replenished, along with a jug of beer. She downed her Love on the Rocks as if it was red lemonade. 'Oops, I'm thirsty,' she said.

One of Chloe's friends poured her a beer. 'There you go, Dancing Queen.'

Jess blushed.

'Yeah, get you Jess, throwing some moves,' said Chloe admiringly.

'I just... haven't been out dancing for a while.'

'Hey, we're going clubbing after. You in?'

Jess hesitated at a night with these uber-cool strangers. But dance was in her blood now.

'Please, pretty please. You know you're my wing-man tonight. Wing-woman.'

Chloe reached across. Her manicured nails flashed a flat-lining heart. 'Someone's got to get me home in time, Jess. My coach is at ten tomorrow.'

'Okay, I'm in.'

So Jess was playing Big-Sis now which rather pleased her. She'd never had a sister but hadn't Greg dubbed her 'Little Miss Sensible' all those years ago? She shook him off. No way was her mother's psycho-boyfriend gonna muscle in on this evening. 'Fuck sensible for once,' she thought. She'd done that for six years. Ever since she moved in with Nan for her GCSEs, then started temping. At 21, her teenage partying was long overdue. She stood up, downed her beer and swayed slightly.

'Right, I'll get you home - on condition you hit the dance-floor, pronto.'

Chloe laughed. Her silver-sequinned dress caught a swirl of violet-lights and she stepped out in scarlet stilettos. Jess coveted those red shoes as she did everything in Chloe's perfect life. When Chloe claimed her arm like a 'bestie' she felt a surge of elation. They sashayed together into the boogieing crowd, giggling at their own hotness.

Wincing at daylight, Jess awoke with the mother of all hangovers. She squinted at her clock and beside it, the photograph tree, her grandmother's gift for winning a University place. Hung from its silver-plated branches, Nan beamed back. Below Sam, she and her mum pulled giddy faces in a photo-booth snap. The heart-shaped frame encased a smudgy baby Jess. Ashamed, she scrabbled in her knickers drawer for something to cover their gaze. Then she fell over trying to get a leg into her trackie bottoms. But when she peered out onto the landing, there was nobody about.

'Aren't you going home for Reading Week?' Chloe'd asked.

'This is home.'

'If you say so.'

Jess was an Independent Student, 'estranged' as the Finance Office called it. She knew 'home address' was just a tick-box to Chloe but Jess longed for it to be more.

Downstairs there was a heap of wet clothes on the bathroom floor that looked familiar. She must have had a shower last night. It hurt to pee and she took her time. Tangled in the clothes pile, the maroon tights sprawled obscenely like a discarded snakeskin. She stuffed them into the bin in disgust.

Back in the kitchen Jess considered a bowl of cereal. The fridge-door was flagged by Abi's yellow post-it note, 'Last one to leave please throw out milk. Thank you.' Abi was the University's Big Sis. Officially Senior House Resident, she was a Bio-Med third-year, currently hill-walking with her fiancée. Jess pulled out a milk carton and found some Honey-Monster Puffs. But when the puffs started popping in the milk, nausea scared away hunger. Abandoning the bowl, she padded back upstairs.

There was an envelope stuck under her door with Chloe's girlish scrawl. 'Hope you're feeling better Jess. Can you water my plant? Here's a key. See you Tuesday.' Jess let herself into

Chloe's room. She dodged a shaft of light that stabbed at her from half-shut curtains. A mess of clothes that didn't make it into Chloe's packing sprawled on the bed. Her childhood toy, a once-orange Tigger, poked out from the tumble.

'Mummy's Full English will sort me out,' Chloe said.

Jess was getting ripped-up shreds of memory from last night. She'd said something about Nan's eggy-bread. They'd been bonding over borrowed lipsticks and life-saving breakfasts. Gulping down another surge of nausea, she sat on Chloe's bed like a dishevelled Goldilocks. Chloe's notice-board opposite was crammed with Good Luck cards, family photos, two lookalike sisters, school friend selfies, even the ex-boyfriend. A rip-tide of envy knocked Jess over.

'Do you think we should still be mates?' Chloe asked earnestly, as if Jess was an oracle of adulthood. 'Little Miss Sensible', Greg sneered.

'Depends if you can stand it. Harder for the dumpee.'

Jess thought of Sam keeping his head down on her Facebook page. Strictly Friends and occasional fuck-buddies was the new arrangement. She was wearing one of his old t-shirts, comforting as a second skin. But it didn't stop her shaking. Probably dehydration. Sam would have known what to do. He'd have looked after her when she got pissed. But she'd left him behind, just as she'd deserted her mother.

Jess groaned. She wanted to crawl under the lilac lace-patterned covers and burrow into Chloe's life. Tigger stared balefully: Somebody's been sleeping in my bed. Jess said, 'Who the hell made you boss of me?' She hurled one of Chloe's cushions and heard a crash.

She leapt up horrified. Brightly coloured porcelain lay shattered over Chloe's carpet. Jess fled in disgrace. Back in her own room, she buried herself under the Poundstretcher duvet.

Her feet were dancing under a red light. Leopard-spotted legs and scarlet toe-nails. They were dancing up a frenzy as if the music was a swarm that stung. It stopped when a door slammed. In the thickening dark, somebody was breathing jaggedly.

In the night the house was a forest. The photograph tree sprouted a weird canopy of shadow. On the landing an open doorway loomed like a hollow trunk. She dreaded the troll who lurked there, stinking of Stella Artois and fags. But the stairwell treads didn't betray her. She crept between three sofas like fallen logs in the darkened common room. When a techno-bass snarl roared out of the walls, she fled into the bathroom.

It smelt bad there. Last night's clothes starting to rot. Sniffing them, she was startled by a phantom in the bin, mascaraed eyes blinking on a purple-red hide. Jess shuddered and lowered herself to the loo. It still hurt. She needed water and paracetamol. Switching on the bluish sink-light, she raided the cabinet behind the mirror. There was a grubby toothbrush, dandruff shampoo, some aftershave and a tin-foil packet. No razor-blades. She clawed out the last tablet and returned to the kitchen.

Next door's music pounded and growled. A cheesy odour hung over the milk carton and Honey Monsters bowl. Fighting back the taste of bile, she drank a whole pint of water. Then she pulled open a drawer. She stood shaking, unsure what she was looking for. She laid out three knives on the work-top. Bread-knife, steak-knife, vegetable knife. She tested each blade in turn. Too blunt. Who's been eating my dinner? Wolf-music circled. She considered her pale, virginal wrist. A girl she knew said cutting stopped pain better than paracetamol. But if she made one gash, she'd never be able to stop.

'It's an addiction,' her mother said. The bruise on her arm was a faded purple eye. 'Love is an addiction.'

Jess begged her but she shrugged. Cupid is stupid.

'I can't, baby. Don't ask me to give him up.'

So Jess left her, moved in with Nan. Just for her GCSE revision, they said but then Greg banned all visits, all contact. He cast her as the ungrateful daughter and her mother was locked in the tower-block, love-gagged. Her Prince jangled the keys, confiscated her mobile.

Now the howling techno-pack was closing in. The three knives smiled. She yanked open the doors under the sink. A dust-pan and brush. A spare basin. A tin that dribbled dark paint. She dragged it out, used one of the grinning knives to force it open. A chemical odour cut through her nausea, scorched her throat. It was red, like half of the student-house doors on the street. Alternate post-box red or ivy green. In a bluish shaft of bathroom twilight, this was the colour of poisonous berries.

She stirred it with the bread-knife. Viscous and delicious, it spilled into the basin like a scarlet woman's blood. The paint slicked coolly as she stepped in, her heart's chamber emptying into her feet. Crimson fumes rose and muffled the music. When she lifted her stumps out, the gloss was tightening to leather. Where she walked, it stamped a gory track. Red feet dancing across the lino forever.

Days passed, duvet-smothered. In her cave of sleep, the same dream. Under a red-spotlight, her bare feet danced like flames leaping, crackling. The music scorched. Her dance demon was in full possession. So tight was its grip, the feet blistered. A bruise winked purple-eyed on her calf but the toes smouldered white. Then a black steel-capped boot crunched down, snuffed out the music. In the dark an animal grunted, pawing.

Jess heard screaming, thought she was home. She sat up, struggling to identify the room. Papa Bear said, 'Who's been hiding in our house?' Screaming turned to shouting and feet clattered on the stairs. She leapt out of bed and cowered, fists raised. The door burst open.

'What the fuck?'

Chloe strode in, an avenging angel in sportswear. Jess staggered backwards.

'What the fuck, Jess?' Chloe repeated. 'Paint everywhere, a knife on the floor. I thought it was blood.'

The word scythed the air between them.

'Did somebody break in? My door's wide open.'

But a line of red prints tracked the guilt to Jess' feet. The paint was muddy now and cracked. She crumpled onto the bed. 'I couldn't find razors.'

'You're scaring me, Jess. Did somebody do this to you?'

'Not here. The club.'

'The nightclub? Matt said you threw up.'

'The man at the door. He did.' She shivered. 'Put me in a taxi.'

'You're making no sense.' Chloe frowned. 'Okay. I give up.' She marched downstairs.

Jess cradled her feet like red secrets. Then she hastily removed the knickers from the photograph tree.

'Don't tell anybody,' her mother had said. 'Don't bring trouble to our door.'

Only Sam knew about the bruises and shouting in that disordered house. Their noisy sex in the next room. Years after, when Jess had nightmares, Sam would whisper, 'It's all right, Jess. I've got you,' till she woke up safely.

'Jess?' Chloe's call interrupted her uneasy stupor. 'Why don't you come into mine?'

She tip-toed out, dodging the footprints as Chloe had done. In her room, Chloe was tidying clothes away, pulling curtains.

'Those wet things of yours smelt rank, Jess. I threw them in the machine.'

'Oh sorry, sorry.' Jess dithered in the doorway.

In a trice Chloe's room looked cosy again. Until she stepped around her bed into the crunch of pottery. Jess stiffened in horror.

'Nooo, my Ariel figurine!' Chloe wailed. 'Mummy gave me this years ago.'

Jess imagined jagged mermaid-shards slicing her feet. Another broken girl.

'Who did this?'

'I didn't break in. You gave me the key.'

'To water my plant.'

Jess's eyes searched for the house-plant. On the window-ledge, its glossy green leaves budded with pink flowers. Miraculously, she hadn't killed it.

'It was an accident Chloe, honestly. I don't know how…'

She flinched as her house-mate rose to drop turquoise pieces into her bin. Chloe paused there. Then she steered Jess to two mugs on the desk.

'Black,' she said, as if it was step-mother's poison.

'Oh. Thanks.'

'Milk's gone off. It was left out,' Chloe said pointedly. She settled herself on a floor-cushion.

Jess sat, a nervous Goldilocks, longing to flee. Someone has smashed my chair. The tea was bitter-sweet.

'So I phoned Abi. I thought, she'll know what to do, right?'

Jess winced at the thought of Abi examining her red foot-prints.

'Shall we do this then?' Chloe asked briskly

Jess followed her sideways glance to a washing-up bowl.

'Oh, I'm not sick.'

'No, Jess. I have to clean up your feet.'

Chloe produced a family-sized bottle of cooking oil. 'Abi said it won't hurt with this. See?' She tipped it into the bowl and the yellow oil glowed like a magic lamp.

'Why don't you put your foot in, Jess?'

Chloe smiled grimly. Jess sucked in a gulp of air and lowered one foot gingerly. Yellow light slid under the arch.

'And the other one,' Chloe said. 'Now we leave that for a while.'

Jess imagined the oil illuminating her skin, turning her hair golden. But then she saw her feet weeping blood into the yellow. She yelped.

'Sit down Jess. It's working.'

Jess cringed. The red slick was gobbling yellow globules. A chemical stink rose. She gagged.

'Okay darling, out you come...' That voice rough as day-old stubble and his acrid whiff of aftershave.

'It won't hurt,' Chloe said. She produced a flannel but hesitated. 'Abi says I've got to scrub it clean.'

Jess leaned back, her head buzzing. The oil's fat-and-gloss odour collided with Chloe's perfume. Her stomach lurched again.

'You were talking about the nightclub earlier...'

'No, no I wasn't.'

'Okay, whatever. This all right?'

Chloe swabbed Jess' paint-scarred foot with the flannel. Tiny splashes of oil tinkled.

'But that bouncer that put you in the taxi...'

'Some fresh air for you, little missy,' he'd promised. He bundled her under his huge arm, half walked, half-carried her from the dancing crowds.

'Don't,' Jess murmured.

Her battered foot wriggled in Chloe's grasp.

'Hang on. Almost there…'

Jess squirmed, nearly tipping the bowl. Chloe let go but quickly fished out the other foot from the bloody spill. She clamped it on her knee with one arm. Jess whimpered.

A door shut out the music except for a thudding beat. No fresh air, no room to push him away. Only smothering darkness and the black door he pressed her into, face first…

Jess jerked her foot away, heaving noisily. She aimed at the red mess in the bowl but for all the hawking, nothing came but a dribble of spit.

'Don't cry Jess, hush,' Chloe soothed. 'You're alright sweetie. Let me just go and empty this.'

Nausea ebbed away as the odour followed Chloe. Jess felt wetness on her face. A sob burst through and subsided. She sprawled exhausted.

Then Chloe was back, smoothing something into Jess' ruined feet. A smell she remembered. Baby-oil, clear as a daughter's tears. Next Chloe eased white tennis socks over her feet like a merciful forgetting.

'All done,' she said. Jess saw her mum kissing a grazed knee when she was little.

'I bet you make a great Big Sis.'

Chloe blushed. 'Abi's the clever one.'

'No, you.'

Chloe smiled. They considered each other like a secret discovered. In that pause Jess felt the golden oil flow between them like an elixir.

'You know Jess, you don't have to tell me anything.'

Jess's feet burned under white cotton.

'But that bouncer you mentioned…'

Chloe's blue eyes searched Jess, sifting the elixir.

'Did he ..?'

Jess waded into that gaze like a pool in a forest clearing. Baby-oil scent wrapped them. She nodded. Chloe's eyes blurred with unshed tears and she looked away. Jess's arms crossed her body.

'Why don't you sleep here tonight sweetie?'

'Like a sleep-over?'

'Yes, if you like. I've got floor-cushions. You can have the bed.'

Relief fought with guilt. Jess didn't trust it. 'Well, if you're sure.'

'Shall I call someone for you?'

Jess grimaced. It cost so much to keep Sam at arm's length. Love bites. Yet he was one who knew how to wake her safely.

'Maybe... He's on my phone. Sam.'

'Okay. You get into bed. You look beat.'

Chloe helped Jess under the covers. Then hugged her, holding on gently.

'You're a mate, Chloe.'

'Yes, I am. We'll get through this together, yeah?'

'Mmn.' Jess yawned in her Little-Bear bed.

'I'll leave the desk-light on. You get some rest, sweetie.'

Chloe disappeared. Tigger grinned lopsidedly, sat on guard. Jess burrowed deeper into the lilac sheets. Trouble was packing its bag of terrors and heading her way. But tonight Chloe would dispatch the landing troll. Her feet, swathed in Chloe's white socks, wriggled a little, then dreamt of stillness.

Down Here
Lee Glenwright

It's dark down here.

I shouldn't complain, it's probably for the best really. Light isn't too good for me anyway. I remember way back, a long time ago, when it made me hurt really bad. It burned my eyes making them feel like they'd pop right out of my skull, while my skin would itch and go red, boiling and peeling away like old tissue paper. An 'All-er-gy', that's what my Mum called it. That's probably why she keeps me away from it all. She just wants me to be safe down here. Safe from the bad 'allergy'.

That's what I like to tell myself. It's the easiest thing to believe, and it's okay most of the time. It's usually pretty quiet except for the noise from above, muffled and hollow. There are no windows and the only way in or out is a hatch set into the low ceiling, locked from the other side. The stairs leading down are made of old wood, all bare and splintered. If you step on them they creak like the dry bones of an old person, like they could just give out and fall apart at any moment. I've tried it once before, but I wound up getting a long splinter in my foot. It didn't really hurt that much, but I screamed anyway. It seemed like a normal sort of way to behave, the kind of thing that people do. So there I was jumping around, howling like some wild animal, until Mum came running down those stairs, looking like she'd fall and break her neck. There was a look on her face that I'd seen many times before. Her skin was almost grey like old candle wax and her eyes and mouth were huge dark circles. She looked frightened. She looks that way a lot of the time.

'What is it? What's wrong?' she gasped, her voice all wheezing and high. When I showed her the splinter hanging out of my foot, she took my shoulders and shook me. 'You have to calm down,' she said, 'or the neighbours will hear and we can't afford to move again. Not right now. Please Billy.'

Moving from place to place. That's something we've done a few times. But everywhere looks pretty much the same to me. The only thing that ever really changes is the name.

The cellar is damp and smells sickly sweet, like moist earth and tree roots. My sense of smell, like my eyesight, is pretty good. I suppose that they both have to be. It's usually really dingy, the only light coming from a naked bulb hanging down from the ceiling that swings to and fro whenever someone tramples on the floor above. When they do it sounds like the whole earth is shaking, dust falls down from the floorboards in little clouds that whirl around the place as they fall. I try and keep out of the way when that happens, it dries my throat up and makes me feel thirsty.

Mum comes down here quite often, her tread is always soft on the stairs. I can never quite tell if that's just because she's so light, or if she's on tiptoe, creeping her way down as if she's afraid of something, even though there's no one else down here except me.

Sometimes when she talks to me, her voice is soft and sweet. Along with the damp smell of the cellar it reminds me of the rain, though I don't know why as I don't think I've ever actually seen rain, I just seem to remember it, as if I'm remembering something that happened to someone else a long time ago. She's so pretty, with her pale skin and her long golden hair. I don't think I look anything like her. Perhaps I look like Dad. I wouldn't know, as I've never seen him. I've heard him though, plenty of times. He shouts and he stomps around, all loudness and anger. They argue a lot. I think it's usually about me.

I've tried asking Mum if I'll ever be free, if I'll ever be allowed outside to see other people. The last time I asked her, she got this look in her eyes, like she'd spotted something far away and it had made her sad. She went quiet for a good while, thinking about the right thing to say as she sat on the edge of my worn old mattress. I thought she was going to get up and walk away, when she let out a long sigh.

'Soon,' she said. 'I promise.'

But I've learned that promises aren't always kept.

They argued shortly after. I heard them. Two voices, hers soft, almost like she was begging, his rough and nasty, growing louder and angrier. Every time she tried to speak he interrupted, as if he didn't want to listen to her. I heard some of the words and they made my stomach hurt.

'No way', he said. 'Keeping him safe' and 'we're only just starting to settle down', he said as well.

I could still hear them later. I put my head under my pillow to try and make it stop, but my hearing is way too good for that. Dad was still shouting, his voice echoing down through the floor, making the ceiling shake:

'Can't risk it.'

'But he's still so young and he's never been out…'

'Yes, but you know what would happen. He's getting stronger all the time. He'll outlive us all, then what? Tell me woman, what then?'

'But he doesn't know that.'

'Not now, but he will. Oh God, he will.'

'We can protect him!'

'But who'll protect us?'

'He's our son, damn it! You're speaking like he's some kind of a monster!'

'Maybe he is. Maybe you shouldn't have done it.'

I bury my head further under the pillow and hum to myself, making any sort of noise to try and drown out their voices. It nearly helps, but not quite. Instead I can just hear a mushy mix of sounds, Dad's shouts and Mum's pleading turning into a mess that just makes my head hurt even more. It goes on for ages and ages, until Mum comes down the creaking steps, in that frightened way again. Always so frightened.

She sits on the end of my my mattress and I can tell that she's upset. Her breathing is loud and she even smells scared, the odour of her sticking in the air. I act like it isn't choking me, when really it feels like it almost is.

'Are you awake?' she asks, like she's hoping I won't answer, her voice even smaller than usual. I pretend that she's woken me up, yawning and opening my eyes, when I wasn't really even tired. I've never even told her that I don't feel tired at the normal times any more.

'Sorry,' she says when I sit up and stretch my arms out. She looks even worse than she sounded, like she might cry, or like she has been already.

'It's okay Momma,' I say, trying to make her feel better, knowing that it's something to do with me, the reason why she's so sad.

'Your Dad and me, we had a bit of a... talk,' she says, thinking that I didn't hear them.

'What about?' I ask her, still pretending that I don't know, trying to find out if she'll tell me the truth or just make something up.

'Oh, you know, stuff,' she says, sighing again. 'Your Dad, he just gets upset sometimes. He just needs a bit of time to calm down.'

'Is it 'cause of me?' I ask her. I look right at her, so I can tell whether or not she means what she says. I'm pretty good at that most of the time. She gets a weird look on her face, like she's looking for the right thing to say.

'It's just a bit difficult for him,' she says. 'He doesn't come down here to see you like I do, so he doesn't know as much as me.' She reaches out and touches the side of my face. Her hand is warm and soft and it feels nice. She pulls it back again quickly, as though she's brushed against something really cold. She gasps as she does so and I don't know if it's because she's shocked or because she's ashamed that she did it. Either way, she reaches back out again and strokes my hair, trying to make it all better.

'Why don't I go fix you something to eat?' She says, smiling at me, 'I'm guessing you could probably do with it.' I nod my head, even though I don't feel hungry.

She turns and walks back up the stairs, missing out the third and fifth steps that creak the worst, as if she doesn't want Dad to know what she's doing. After a couple of minutes she comes back down, just as quietly. She's carrying the usual shiny metal bowl. It catches the light, all gleaming and new-looking. She sets it down on the bed in front of me.

'There you go son,' she says, her voice calmer now, more gentle. 'It's just like a midnight snack.' She turns and walks away again, like she doesn't want to watch me eat. I scoop the chunks of food up with my hands and cram them into my mouth. They're cold and chewy and I wonder if it's the kind of stuff they eat upstairs. When I bite down on the pieces the sauce squirts out and dribbles down my chin, making it sticky. It's my favourite part, so I wipe it off and suck it from my fingers, not wanting to waste any of it. After a couple of minutes the buzzing noise in my head stops. Maybe I was hungry after all.

Or maybe the sound was just caused by another one of those allergy things.

Once I'm done I lick the last bits of thick, gloopy sauce out from the bottom of the bowl, before putting it down at the bottom of my mattress. I lie down and put my pillow over my head for a bit, just in case Dad starts shouting again.

More shouting. It's getting worse. It's Dad again, but he sounds different, even louder than usual, and his voice sounds all slow and thick, as if something's happened to stop him getting the words out right and it's making him more angry.

'...Told you before, we can't cope like this!'

'...Wish you'd try and help me face up to things rather than go out and get wasted...'

'Damn it, you bitch! The hell with you!'

There's a loud noise, like something being thrown and broken. Then another. And another. Mum starts to cry, but she still sounds angry too.

'That's your answer to everything, isn't it? Always is. Just keep moving, keep on hiding away.'

What else is there to do? Go on! Tell me!'

'We could let him out, try and teach him.'

More breaking noises. Dad must be really mad.

'You kidding? You really are crazy!'

There's a really loud crash, then another. Mum screams and Dad shouts, a really low noise, like nothing I've heard before. It's pretty scary.

'He's stronger than both of us put together and it's only a matter of time before he knows it. And then what, you stupid bitch?'

Mum screams really, really loud. No words, just screaming. Then Dad shouts like he's been given a really nasty surprise. I'm just about to jump off the mattress and shout at them both to stop, when there's a loud crashing thump, right above me. It sounds really bad, as though the ceiling is going to fall down on me. A cloud of dust comes from the floorboards above, then everything goes quiet, quieter than I've ever heard before.

After a while everything goes dark.

The big darkness doesn't happen very often. That's probably why it feels so bad when it does. It's like I'm stuck in a really, really black place with no light and no way of moving or escaping. I think it's probably something to do with not having any food or drink. Maybe it's the worrying about stuff that makes it worse.

Mum touches the side of my face, every bit as softly as usual. I open my eyes to look at her. She's pale and her hand's shaking just a little. But for some reason, I don't think it's because of me this time. She speaks to me and her voice is quiet and fluttery. It floats toward me from out of the darkness.

'You've been sleeping for a while,' she says, 'you must be hungry.'

She passes me my metal bowl. It's full of thick liquid, sloshing up the sides, she almost spills it as she hands it over.

'Careful. I've warmed it for you,' she says. I grip the metal with both hands and take great big gulps from it. It tastes sweet and salty at the same time, and it warms my insides as I swallow it down, making the buzzing in my ears go away again. I don't even wonder about where she got it from. I don't really care, I just know that it makes me feel better, makes me forget everything bad.

Mum sits there, watching me drink. She turns away, just for a moment, when I wipe the dribbles from my chin, feeling its warmth as it smears my ice cold skin, licking the last of it from my fingers. I grunt at her in thanks, holding the empty bowl out for her to take. She sets it down on the floor next to her feet. She gives a long sigh.

'I think we're going to have to move again, Billy,' she says, her voice soft and quiet. She reaches out her hand again, as if to comfort me. I look at her, and I know that I don't have to tell her how I feel. She already knows.

'That means The Box, right?' I ask, hoping that she'll change her mind.

'Yes, that means The Box,' she says, nodding her head. 'It won't be for long, Bill, I promise. Just until we find some place new.' She stops, sighing again. 'Dad won't be coming with us,' she says. 'He's stopping here for a while, just while the rest of us get settled.' I can't really tell if she's lying or not. I'm too busy thinking about The Box, so small and cramped, with its smell of damp cellar earth, me having to lie in there away from the light. Always hiding.

'Mum, are you down there with him?' A low voice comes down the stairway and Mum's face changes. She suddenly looks really afraid. She stands and runs up the wooden steps, not bothered about the noise for the first time in a long while. The stairs creak and sag that fifth one almost collapsing. The light comes through the hatch and I can see someone a lot like Mum, but younger, with long blonde hair, looking like I think an angel might. That's all I get to see before Mum closes the hatch. I hear the voice again, full of curiosity.

'Why did he look like that, all thin and grey? And he still looks like he's the same age as me.'

'That's because they don't really sparkle, except in stories,' I hear Mum say, her voice sad. Always so sad. There's a loud scraping noise as she forces the heavy bolt back into place.

Count Von Cosel's Great Love
Douglas Ford

Years later, no one would believe they had lined up to see the dead face of Elena de Hoyos. Of course, they wanted to see, but they hardly anticipated the school letting out just for that purpose, that glimpse. They'd heard their parents talk about what happened in hushed tones, stories of the man who'd built the mausoleum for Elena nine years ago, only to secretly remove her body to restore her rotted flesh with oiled silk and clothe her in a wedding gown. They wanted to see what he did to her, her face now mostly plaster and wax, her limbs held together with coat hangers and piano wire. The teachers wanted to see, too, so they all went.

Trish Fallbrook tried to fathom the decay under all that work. She stood in line behind Ron Wiley, the kid who delivered groceries to the home of the man who called himself Count Von Cosel, not his real name, but the name he took when he left his home country for Key West. Ron liked to tell everyone about how he saw the Count dancing with someone through the curtains, twirling around the room like he had a waltz going, only he heard no music, even as he got closer and closer because he wanted to see. When he did, he thought the Count had a big doll, and he wondered why a grown man would play with dolls.

Then talk got around their small island and soon, people found out what the Count had done because he loved Elena so much. They already knew how sad he felt when she died because he built that mausoleum for her, the one where he put the phone so he could talk to her even though she was dead. Trish overheard some of the other kids, the ones from the Methodist Youth Group, talking about how he'd built a phone that could call heaven. She thought that sounded stupid, and she must have said so out loud without realizing it.

Ron heard her. 'He wanted her to talk to him pretty bad,' he said. 'But how can you talk when you're rotting? That's probably why he put her back together. So she could talk again.'

'Maybe she was done talking,' Trish said.

Six students stood between her, Ron and the casket. Everyone seemed to take a long time looking at Elena's dead face, and when Trish finally got close enough, she could see why.

Elena no longer looked like a real person. Count Von Cosel had used so much wax and plaster to cover her sunken features that her head looked round and bloated. With painted lips and eyebrows drawn grotesquely over depth-less glass eyes, she looked artificial, not the beautiful sixteen-year-old girl that he fell in love with in the hospital. A doll's face, she thought.

'Go ahead, said Ron. 'Ask her if she has anything to say.'

'Shut up,' Trish said, but she found herself leaning closer to the face in the casket, wondering if she did hear something coming from the mouth held together by wires and sealed shut with wax.

There's a skull underneath all that, Trish thought. The brain has rotted away. She learned that somewhere, that the brain decayed first when a person died, and she wondered if an echo remained, calling out in the hollow space left behind. A person lived here once.

A decade ago, they said, Elena was the belle of the island, her beauty envied and craved, even by someone as old as Count Von

Cosel. He worked in the hospital where her parents brought her, desperate to stop her from coughing up blood, and even after she died he had plans, she heard, to bring her back to life. He couldn't accept her death, so he wanted to use an airship to take her up into the sky where the radiation of the sun would reanimate her. Until then, the best he could do now lay in this coffin, here in the funeral home, where people wanted to see it. Trish leaned closer and closer, reaching out finally to touch the lips, the cheek, to see if she could feel the echo she sensed in there. The face felt harder than she expected.

'Miss, don't hold up the line. And refrain from touching Miss Hoyos, please.'

Trish did feel a vibration in her fingers, but it went away when she heard this. It came from the funeral home director, a man in a black suit. She straightened her back and looked at him.

'Why are you doing this?' she said. 'Putting her out like this so everyone can stare at her. She doesn't like it. She doesn't like it at all.'

'You mean of course that you don't like it,' the man said. 'Please, move along and leave Miss Hoyos in peace. We honour and respect the dead here. And the love they inspire.'

'She doesn't like it?' Ron said when they stood on the sidewalk outside. 'You're one spooky girl, Trish.'

The fingers that touched Elena's face bore white flecks of plaster, or perhaps paint. Had he painted her?

'People gawking at her like that, and I'm the spooky one,' said Trish. She wiped her fingers against her skirt. 'I'm not the one who dug her up and put all that on her.'

'You're going to love tomorrow then,' said Ron. 'We got a guest speaker coming to class. Guess who owes a favour to Mrs. Stitcher? The romantic old wizard himself. We get to hear all about how he did it and why he plays with dolls.'

Trish didn't answer. Those flecks on her fingers wouldn't come off, no matter how hard she rubbed.

At home, Trish began boxing up all her dolls. They all reminded her of Elena's face, and she knew she'd find sleep impossible that night with them all staring at her. Her father smoked his pipe and congratulated her on her initiative.

'About time,' he said. 'How long have I been saying that you're too old for these?'

He stood just outside the door of her room, not crossing the threshold. Since she started wearing a bra, he had refrained from hugging her and started acting like an invisible force field protected her room, one specially designed to keep fathers out. She felt constantly weird around him now.

He watched as she bagged each plastic doll for him to take up to the attic later. Under his gaze, she resisted speaking to each doll, assuring them that she would not forget them. Thinking of them bunched up there in the attic made her think of that book she had to read for school, 'Jane Eyre', and the madwoman, Mrs. Rochester, forced to make a home of her attic prison. That in turn made her think of Elena pressed into her mausoleum, and that made her feel worse, even though she knew you couldn't make a dead person a prisoner. Not really.

That night, moonlight cut through her curtains, and the shelves in her room glowed in their bareness. She struggled to stay asleep, awakening several times to see an empty wooden bench next to the bed. Each time, she started at that emptiness, so used to her dolls sitting there that she wondered for an instant where they had gone, until she turned on to her side and shut her eyes tightly, angry at herself for doing something so impulsive and childish. She wanted them back. Her father was stupid. She was stupid.

At one point, she swore she could feel the return of their reassuring presence, that sense of protection they seemed to provide and the whole reason she found it hard to give them up in the first place. But when she opened her eyes, she didn't see the dolls at all.

She saw the chalky, unreal face of Elena de Hoyos, sitting where the dolls used to be, as if she had silently climbed down from the attic to join Trish in her bedroom, just like mad Mrs. Rochester, bent on setting the house on fire.

Trish didn't scream at first. She thought of what Ron said, how it looked like Count Von Cosel was dancing around his room with a large doll. It seemed for an instant like all the dolls had joined together to form Elena.

She wore what looked like a wedding dress, her painted saucer eyes seeing and not seeing at the same time. She wanted Trish to look lower. She spread her legs and lifted the dress, and when Trish saw what she had there, she screamed and screamed until her father came running and turned on her light.

'What?' her father said as light filled the room. Trish couldn't stop screaming even though the wooden bench where she'd seen Elena now sat empty. 'What?' her father said again, from the doorway, not daring to come into her room, which now felt like a tomb.

'Did she feel much pain?'

A girl from the Methodist Youth Group asked Count Von Cosel this question after he finished lecturing. He had to wait for a few chuckles to subside before answering. He smiled in a way that made Trish feel sick. A grey beard, carefully trimmed, lent an aura of authority to his appearance, and he looked around the classroom with eyes magnified by round glasses.

They seemed to settle on Trish when he answered. She hardly slept at all the night before, and even if it showed in her face, she still felt wide awake.

'I know what they don't know.' She wished he could hear her thoughts. Then she could read the truth of it in his face. She would know it for sure, the awful truth that the apparition concealed under its dress. 'I know what you did,' she almost said aloud. 'She lifted her dress and showed me.'

Count Von Cosel held her gaze long enough for her to wonder if he could hear those thoughts. Surely not, no more than he could hear the dead speak.

'Are you really asking me if death hurts? Please, I've come here to talk about science. The lovely Mrs. Stitcher tells me you want to learn about the radiation in our atmosphere and how it can rejuvenate dead cells and tissues.' Mrs. Stitcher smiled at the compliment. She sat at her desk, leaning forward as if she wanted to eat each word he spoke out of the air. 'I know this from many years working in my field. Do you all know what I did for a profession? How I first met Elena? How I first met Mrs. Stitcher?'

Ron raised his hand. 'The guy who runs the X-ray machines.'

Trish watched for Mrs. Stitcher's reaction and saw the smile. Their teacher had already told the class about how he helped her with her injured hip. The way she spoke of it made it sound like he'd run his hands all over her body, and she'd loved every minute of it.

'Yes, precisely, a technologist,' said Count Von Cosel, 'and I made it my life's mission to learn about how such things as radiation shape our cosmos and our being. From such things we derive our very lives. Do you all know of my laboratory?'

Everyone nodded. They all knew where to find the wingless air plane fuselage the count had fashioned into a laboratory, behind the Marine Hospital where he once worked. Where he had taken Elena and put her back together the way he did.

'I would like to extend an invitation to each and every last one of you to come visit me in my laboratory. There, I can show you how such things work.'

'I heard that you're going to jail,' said another Youth Group girl, a friend of the first girl. She didn't wait to be called on and would hear it from Mrs Stitcher later.

Count Von Cosel took off his glasses and began wiping them with a handkerchief. 'True. My trial begins soon. But I believe my testimony will more than exonerate me. They will return Elena's body to me. She will come back to me. Either that, or no one shall have her. No one. And the mausoleum where she once lay - no more it will be.'

Even Mrs. Stitcher looked less comfortable now. She opened her mouth to say something but Trish spoke first, not raising her hand. 'Does death hurt?'

Count Von Cosel stopped rubbing his glasses and looked at her, saying nothing. Mrs. Stitcher opened her mouth again, but she remained silent too.

'You should use that phone in the mausoleum,' said Trish, 'and ask her what it feels like.' She thought of what she saw in her bedroom the night before and how Elena showed her the tubes coming out of her body. Coming from the place down there.

When he answered, Count Von Cosel's voice became very quiet, as if everyone except Trish had suddenly vanished. 'Oh, I have spoken with her,' he said. 'And I've asked her. She's said things to me you could never imagine. She's even sung to me. A Spanish song.'

The count went on to explain the electrical principles behind how any telephone worked and how it stood to reason that it could pick up the voices of the dead. 'Have you all not at one point picked up the receiver and heard voices you did not recognize?' All a matter of science, of course, when you considered how the human consciousness amounted to nothing more than wave patterns, electricity. 'The soul is like a radio signal.' So it stood to reason that life, under the right conditions, could return to the body, 'Like re-charging a battery'. But Trish barely heard, her attention fixated on the Count's eyes, magnified once again by the glasses, and the way they never seemed to leave her face.

'Are you going, or not?' Ron said. He pestered Trish as they walked home that afternoon. Since the school trip to the funeral home, he pestered her quite a bit. Now, he wanted her to join the group that planned to visit the Count's laboratory.

'For the last time, no,' she said. She slowed her pace, hoping he would walk ahead, but he slowed with her.

'Afterwards, we could go somewhere. I'm talking about just you and me.' He lowered his voice. 'I know places.'

'You said I was spooky,' she said.

'You are. I like that. Especially today. What was all that about?'

She frowned and looked in the direction of Solares Hill, where the Old Town residents of Key West buried their dead. If Ron would just walk on, she would make her way in that direction.

'I don't like what he did,' she said. 'Everyone's treating him like he made some grand statement of love, but she didn't love him.'

'I know what you all don't know,' she thought, and for a moment, she almost told Ron about what she saw in her room, how she saw what that man put between Elena's legs so that he could... The thought broke off, not wanting to form.

'I thought it was all in the name of science,' Ron said. 'Hey, do you think Mrs. Stitcher gets friendly with him when her husband's away?'

'She's jealous,' said Trish. 'Of Elena.'

'You think she wants to die so that Count Von Cosel can do all that stuff to her?'

'I know what you all don't know.'

'No. Nobody wants that. Or at least, I don't think anyone wants that.' She stopped walking. She needed to get to the western end of the island and through the cemetery gates before nightfall. 'Look, I have to do something, and I need you to leave me alone.'

'If I can guess what it is,' he said, 'can I come along?'

Trish said no, but he guessed right and came along anyway.

They found the mausoleum at the end of a row of palm trees, a squat house of sloped marble surrounded by smaller granite plots and spires. Because the people of the Old Town had to learn how to live with hurricanes that washed away grave dirt and left beaches strewn with corpses, they let their dead rest above ground, locked away in stone.

On the way, Ron took something out of his pocket, a piece of paper he had folded up.

'You seen this?' he said, letting her hold it. It had come out of a newspaper, a picture of a dark haired woman with full lips. 'It's Elena, before she... you know.'

He let her hold it. 'Why do you have this?'

He shrugged. 'She looks like you, I guess.'

She held on to it and studied it until they reached their destination, trying to find the likeness he saw. But she could see none.

Beside the mausoleum two stone benches welcomed them. Ron sat down and patted the seat next to him, but Trish ignored the invitation so she could walk around and study the structure. 'Just like an attic... or no, not that. It looks like an oven,' she said, regarding the door. 'Like we could open it and pull out a fresh loaf of bread.'

'Or cake,' Ron said. 'Why don't you sit down? I'm tired after all that walking.'

She gave him a stern look and kept exploring. 'I want to find the phone.'

As if he already knew where to find it, Ron pointed toward her feet, and yes, in the brush that had grown against the side, she found a plain phone sitting, as if cast aside, a wire extending from it and into the wall of the structure. She hesitated before picking it up. She wanted it to work, at the same time refusing to believe it could. No, she corrected herself, she didn't want it to work. Ron still sat on the bench, watching her. She imagined Count Von Cosel sitting like that, waiting for Elena to sing to him.

'Talk into it,' Ron said. 'See if she's there.'

She wished he would leave. The sky turned pink as the sun started to go down. She held the receiver to her ear and began to whisper so he wouldn't hear.

Ron walked over and stood behind her, close enough that her hair touched his face, and she felt something hard as his hips pressed into her. She inched away from him, though he appeared not to notice or care. 'What's she saying?'

'I don't hear anything,' Trish said. But that wasn't true. Pressing the receiver closer to her ear, she thought she heard a faint, muffled sound, almost singing. A flock of gulls flew overhead, calling out to each other. Could she have heard them in the distance?

'Can I try?' Ron said.

She held the phone away from him. Working or not, it had become a thing to protect, but none of that seemed to matter to Ron. When she wouldn't give up the phone, he went to the door of the tomb and knocked. 'Are you there, Elena?' he called. 'Did Count Von Cosel leave anything behind for us to talk to? An ear maybe?' He pretended to wait for an answer and said, 'She says to come in.'

Before she could tell him not to, he tried the door.

'It's not locked,' he said, opening it and gazing inside. She leaned in too, at the same time trying to keep some distance from him.

Part of her expected to find a dark haired woman inside, singing back to her on another phone. Instead, the stone slab they encountered lay vacant, and the tomb looked all the more like an oven to Trish. Just missing a flame and a long, slender stick to pull the bread out. 'Or a witch,' she thought, 'waiting to push them in and set them on fire.'

'The wire just goes into nothing,' Ron said. He turned to her, and she instinctively took a step back. He cocked his head. 'Did you hear that?'

'Like singing?' As soon as she said this, Trish wished she hadn't.

'You did hear something,' Ron said. 'I knew you were lying. I could see it in your face.'

'It was just birds.'

'How do you know?' They both stood up straight. 'How about this: you crawl in, and I'll stay out here and use the phone. Let's see if we can talk to each other that way.'

'I'm not getting in there,' she said.

'Think of it as an experiment.'

She shook her head but felt the impulse to do it. She wanted to, even before he suggested it. She looked around them. The sky continued to darken, and no one else was in the cemetery.

'Just for a moment,' he said. 'I'll help you get in and out.'

'Ok, a short moment,' she said.

He agreed and actually held out his hand, expecting her to shake it to seal the pact, not to avoid it like she did. His lips pouted as he opened the tomb door wider for her to climb in.

Inside the air was hot and damp, but she forced herself to climb all the way in. Even though she could sit up on the raised floor, it felt stifling and cramped, and she turned to remind Ron that she wouldn't stay long, only to find him climbing in behind her. 'I just want to see what it's like in here,' he said.

'You can try it alone. When I'm done.'

'We can both fit. Do you think that's what he did? Crawled in here with her, his doll?'

She put her hand on his shoulder and pushed, feeling the sweat through the fabric of his shirt. In the dimming light, his eyes looked blank and lifeless.

'We don't have time,' she said, 'and I don't want... this.'

'You're a spooky girl. I thought you'd like to get in here with me.'

The scent of his breath reached her, rich and pungent. She shook her head, unable to believe he would think that. But her mind returned to the hard spot in his pants and how eager he seemed to find the tomb with her, not to help her try the phone, but to get her inside.

'I need you to get out,' she said. 'I can't breathe with you in here.'

'Just lie back and close your eyes. Imagine you're her. I'll pretend to be him. You pretend to be dead.'

'I can't... won't.' Her breath came in short, shallow gasps now. His slouched body blocked the door to the mausoleum, barring her way out. She couldn't crawl over him and she didn't want to. She thought of how Elena appeared in her room and what she showed Trish between her legs, the tubes that Count Von Cosel put up her body so he could defile it, the corpse that couldn't protest. She couldn't stop the thought: how Count Von Cosel had done more than keep her limbs wired together and her cheeks from caving in. The phrase her father used when their dog got out and on top of the neighbor's collie flooded her imagination: 'Relations'. He had 'relations' with her.

'I didn't see just dancing, you know,' Ron said. Even with the darkness creeping in, she could see his teeth when he smiled. 'I saw him slide it in.' The word itself smelled rancid when he spoke it. 'Slide.' That snake of tubing winding its way up her collapsing body, keeping her whole so he had something to slide into.

She could have screamed. She wanted to. But she tried speaking softly instead.

'Please, can we try the phone first?'

Ron didn't reply at first. She could hear him breathing through his mouth.

'You want to see if it works in here?' he said, finally. 'See if you can hear me?'

'Yes.'

'Then you'll lie back and close your eyes?'

She tried to keep her voice from breaking. If she hurried, she could crawl out while he went to pick up the phone. 'Yes.'

More breathing sounds, and underneath that her own heart beating.

'OK,' he said. She held back as he worked his way out of the tomb, knowing she had to time it right. Standing, he looked back at her, a square of purple in the near absence of light. 'Only I don't believe you,' he said, and shut the door.

Panting, she crawled to it and began pushing, but he pressed his weight against it from the other side, keeping it from opening. She could hear him fumbling with something and she realized he had a lock of some kind.

'You need to stay in there for a little while,' he said, his voice muffled by the walls. 'Cook for a bit. Get the right moistness. Soften a little. Let the worms chew on you for a while before I come back.'

Banging on the door, she screamed his name in the darkness. From outside, he replied with laughter and his muffled voice shifted and moved. 'He's walking around the mausoleum,' she realized. She imagined him picking up the phone and pretending to talk to her, mocking her. She screamed his name again, and it came to her, a kind of singing in a faint voice. She came to the awful conclusion that he was dancing and singing around her. Her screaming became a kind of wail, then a low moan, that allowed her to hear more clearly. It occurred to her that the singing came from behind her.

With her. Inside the tomb.

She wasn't alone.

Over her shoulder, she saw the face, Elena's impossible face, alight and glowing, and it smiled and sang as Ron continued to laugh and dance outside. It didn't frighten Trisha this time. She wondered if her own friends and family would line up someday to see her desecrated body. A vision came to her: throngs of people wearing masks fashioned in the likeness of Elena de Hoyos, crowded around a vegetable cart bearing Trish's corpse, Ron dancing around, wearing a mask like the rest of them.

'When he comes back for me,' said Trish, 'you'll make sure I'm not alone?'

She meant Ron, but Elena's presence reminded her that another might come first, once the worms started to eat. He would come with his wires and his wax, his lipstick and his tubing, and he would put her back together.

But Elena's song told her of another possibility. She sang of a despondent Count Von Cosel, denied the body of his love, planting explosives around the mausoleum and destroying it so no one else would ever touch it again.

'He won't even know I'm in here,' said Trish, 'will he?'

Yet no answer interrupted the song, and the voice that did not sing for Count Von Cosel then did not sing for Trish now. The woman who shared her grave sang for herself only while Trish would listen as long as the air held, and when the light finally dimmed, it dimmed completely and brutally even as the song continued.

Pigeon Holes
Richard Lakin

She slipped out at ten. She was making a habit of it, my Helen. I'd got so wrapped up in scouring the dishes I'd taken my eye off the ball, so to speak. My hands were pinkish in the steamy water and I shook them out as I slid across the floor of the kitchenette in my socked feet. The draught from the keyhole made me blink and my eye water. After a quick look around, I took off the chain, cradling it in my fingers so it didn't jangle. I stepped out onto the frayed patch of carpet and sniffed. Wisps of black smoke swirled around the bare light bulb meaning Ferris had burnt his toast again. I glanced through the spiral of stair-rods, keeping well back from the edge and the weird wobbly sensation the drop gave me.

It was typical that the only room available had been on the third floor and I'd never managed to escape it. I'd found the room in the local free-sheet and it'd been the only one I could afford. I was met by a bloke with a handshake like a vice, whose roll-ups smelt of creosote. It'd turn out to be one of my few sightings of Ron the Landlord. It couldn't have been more than five past, but he tapped his watch and said, 'I suppose this is what passes as timekeeping for students.' I let that one go and followed him up the creaking stairs trying to look as if I knew what I was doing by peering into cupboards and flicking switches. I hoped that giving him the impression I had a clue about buildings would stop him stitching me up.

'I've got others coming, kid,' Ron said.

I hovered on the landing, fidgeting with the zip on my raincoat, as he locked up. Mother had always been there to make these decisions, but no more. I nibbled at my lip and said I'd take it. Wasn't that daring of me? It wasn't what you call homely but I made the best of it. And then one day my Helen turned up and took the room along the landing.

I sat on the top step. The gap between the stairs gave a familiar view of that patch of lino and the pink bike frame chained to a radiator. I couldn't see Helen, but I heard the rusting key turn and the lock finally give way with a clunk. She shouldered the door where the damp had warped it, and it scuffed against the tiles with a squeal. It was on the long list of jobs Ron was 'getting round to'. There was a rustle from her carrier bag. I closed my eyes and inhaled because sometimes, when I was sitting up here, I got a shot of her perfume if the draught caught it and wafted it up. Bottles clinked against each other, slamming into the side of the bin. She made a right old racket and I think she must've been on my wavelength, trying to scare old Ferris into an early grave so she got his room and saved herself a climb - only joking. Helen had to be drinking three, four times her weekly limit. I wasn't really the type to interfere but I'd posted her a leaflet I'd picked up at the GPs and when it dropped on the mat Ferris or Miss Penrose must've put it in her pigeon hole. It cost me a second-class stamp, but I didn't want her thinking it was me sticking my oar in. The following morning it was gone, but it didn't stop the bottles clinking. She'd taken to drink, I supposed, as most people did, to fill a hole in her life.

I want to help Helen. I want us to be friends. I say Helen because it's the name I've settled on and it fits. Before long I'd ended up sorting the post - someone had to what with the state of the porch - and unclaimed letters were arriving from the Wildlife Trust, Friends of the Earth and the doctors for Ms. Glover, initial H. One day she dropped a multi-coloured scarf on the landing. It was laced with her musky perfume and I thought it suited a Helen perfectly. It's kind of stuck with me since and, to be honest, it fits her like a Glover. Ha!

I'd got the labels off some of her favourite wines, she preferred the New World ones with a hint of spice, perfect with meat dishes. It was easy enough to soak them from the glass and when she came for dinner I knew what to get in from the supermarket. I'd open the wine so it breathed first, of course, and light the church candles so she felt at home, and maybe play some Berlioz.

This wasn't the first time I'd tried, but you know what they say: 'If at first you don't succeed…' It would've been September the sixth I first plucked up the guts to do something. I'd been reading one of the new self-help books in the library and I'd decided it was now or never and I should be bold and go ahead and cook something. I shouldn't even give her the chance to back out. Faint heart ne'er won fair lady and all that.

It had been hammering with rain, streaking the windows, when I set out for the shops. A gust of wind snatched at my umbrella and a van steered in toward the kerb and sent a tide of gutter water up my trouser leg. I was drenched and disheartened and thoroughly ticked off with it all. When the wind got up I lost hold of the umbrella. It turned inside out and broke and I stamped on it in a fit of temper and left it crumpled in the gutter. It was one of those decisive moments and I decided I wasn't going to give up. I bought spinach and pasta and parmesan from the deli counter and a bottle of her preferred red, the brand she liked to save for a Friday night treat. I was dripping when I got in, shaking myself out like a drowned rat. I had to pause on the way up the stairs and catch my breath. I didn't want her to hear me panting at her door like those funny men you read about. She was listening to music, something folky, but so faint I couldn't place it. I was about to knock when I had a better idea. I rummaged around in the craft box I kept on top of the wardrobe and found some gold card and glitter. I folded it so it presented like an invitation and even found a scarlet envelope leftover from Christmas.

I wrote, 'Your neighbour requests your company for dinner - 7 for 7.30pm. RSVP.'

You'll note I didn't write my name. It would be part of the mystery, an aid to conversation as I was sure she was keen to know more. I tucked the card into the envelope and slid it under her door dashing back into my flat on tip-toes. I sat at the table, drumming my fingers and wondering what she'd make of it. Was I being too forward? Would I frighten her off? I yawned and stretched. Adrenalin always made me tired. I hadn't done anything like this since I'd sent a Valentine to Debbie Slater in third year only for it to be snatched by Scott Sykes and passed around to nudges and giggles at assembly. I bit my thumbnail, drawing blood as I watched the space beneath the door waiting for her to RSVP. 'Oh, Helen,' I felt like screaming, 'répondez s'il vous plaît.' The rain kept falling, gusts causing it to sting the window panes. An hour passed. There was no sign of the card, no knock. She'd come, I decided, but she didn't want to seem too keen. So, I dashed inside, ran a bath and had a long, hot soak. I ran the water so it was steaming and got as much of me as I could beneath the surface to avoid the chill. Ron had never got round to tiling the wall, so the plaster was pale pink and crumbling. I left my wet hand print on the plaster and watched it fade before disappearing altogether. I was that hand print. I'd made no mark here, little of a mark in life at all really. There was no sign I'd even lived here save for the dandruff or hairs I shed, or the crumbs I spilt at breakfast that fell through the bare boards. Well, chin up! It was no use thinking like that if I was going to snare Helen's affections. I took the tumbler I used for my toothbrush and cupped it to the wall. Right now, I hoped Helen was doing much the same thing, in readiness for our meal. I closed my eyes and saw her stretch out a foot through the suds and run her fingertips along that smooth, pale skin. I didn't think she wore nail varnish, or if she did it wouldn't be the flash type those women sold in department stores. It would be black or purple, challenging the conventions of her workplace as far as she dared. She was spirited like that, was Helen. She'd wear purple Docs and stripy leggings and she wouldn't be frightened to be herself. I set the glass down. I had no right to intrude. Perhaps a few moments before we'd both held glasses to the same wall wondering why it had gone eerily silent. I jumped out and towelled off. I found some after-shave left over from Christmas. It was the last present Mother had bought me, taunting that it might help break my duck. It was a market copy, the type where they rip off well known makes but change the spelling so it's legal. When I dabbed it on my cheeks it nipped and bit like a paper cut and made me gasp. I'd seen Mother that Boxing Day, a little tradition we'd kept for years. Her cheeks were hollow and pinched. Her hair was wispy and thin and her scalp was like turkey flesh. She clutched her handbag on her lap. The last words she'd said to me, 'I've tried my best for you.' She meant I'd been a disappointment: no grandchildren, no job with a suit, these four walls I called home. The degree she'd funded. 'I can't keep you and no one else will.' I could've told her about Helen but I didn't. I uncorked the wine, fiddled to get the volume right on the stereo so we could enjoy Berlioz without it being intrusive. An hour passed and then another. My collar began to irritate me and then my trousers. I sat watching the candle flicker, fiddling with my cuffs and wetting and smoothing down my fringe. I drank a glass of wine and then another. I stood outside her door but I didn't knock. Finally, I licked my finger-tips and nipped the flame of the candle.

It would've been about a week later and I was climbing the stairs when Miss Penrose came in shaking off her rain bonnet and cussing the weather.

'Oh,' she said. Miss Penrose was active in the church and probably didn't like that I'd heard her cussing. I asked why she'd been out when it was coming down like cats and dogs.

'It's my drawing class,' she said. She had a large spiral bound sketchpad under her arm, but I knew she wouldn't show it to me.

'It'd do you good. It'd put some colour in your cheeks.' There was an awkward silence and I realised Miss Penrose was waiting for me to move.

'Bad luck.' I said, meaning to pass on the stairs and I retreated to the middle landing. She wouldn't accept my offer to help with her shoulder bag and groceries. She fidgeted with her keys, most of the locks requiring a knack she'd never acquired.

'Here let me,' I said.

'No, it's alright.'

I insisted and handed her the post I was holding while I waggled the key in the lock, snapping it this way and that. Finally, I got the door open, said, 'Ta da!' and stood back. She didn't thank me. She was thumbing through the post.

'These aren't yours,' she said.

'Well not all of them. I take care of….'

'But these are for Miss…' She frowned.

I scratched my chin. 'Yeah and I'm taking them up for her.'

Miss Penrose's eyes narrowed.

'Yeah, I thought I'd take them up and…' my voice trailed off seeing she was staring at me, eyes narrowed. Miss Penrose began shaking her head.

'No, no, no. I've been sending her letters on. I take care of that because…'

My throat tightened. 'Sending them on?' Miss Penrose said she was surprised I didn't know.

'Sarah's in Australia. I've been forwarding the important ones on to her.' She made a point of saying Sarah, which only proved she'd got her wires crossed. It was sad to see her losing her marbles already. Or maybe she thought I hadn't clocked the bottle of red she'd tried to secrete behind her veggies. I was surprised and not a little disappointed to note she favoured the same tipple as Helen. She sniffed and said she had things to be getting on with and shut the door leaving me alone on the landing. So, Helen hadn't seen fit to tell me she was off on the holiday of a lifetime, but at least I felt better about the meal. She hadn't intended to stand me up and there'd be other times to break open that wine.

I waited a few more minutes, but the cold was getting to my bones. Whatever she was doing by the bins there was no sign of her coming back upstairs. Perhaps she was short of milk or coffee and had nipped to Karim's. She only had to ask and I'd gladly fetch her groceries. The chimes of the late-night news bonged from my room and I stepped back inside and put a pan of milk on the hob, stretching my fingers before the blue flame. I sipped and blew the steam so it warmed my cheeks and turned the fire up to three bars. I got a tartan blanket, tucked it round my feet and slipped the hot water bottle onto my lap. Everyone else would be doing the same thing, sitting watching the News at Ten and worrying about the murderers and rapists and crooks and cheats out there. When the ads came on I killed the sound, sat back, clasped my hands round the mug and tried not to shiver. There was a creak on the landing. I kicked off the blanket and almost knocked my cocoa flying as I skipped across to the door. I dropped to my knees and stared unblinking through the keyhole. I had a bottle of her preferred Shiraz ready, a link to her recent stint Down Under and a talking point for us no doubt as the evening wore on. It was on the table waiting to be opened with dips and some posh crisps I'd seen advertised. I undid the catch, opened the door gently, cushioning the chain in my hand. There was no sign of her. I stepped out onto the frayed patch of carpet and cupped my ear against her door. The music was faint, so faint.

I came to staring at the green diodes on my alarm clock. Weak daylight poked through the gap in the curtains. I dropped my feet onto the boards and sat rubbing my head, aware of a night-mare, a vague feeling of threat or panic but nothing I could hold onto. My tongue was gummy and my back ached. I padded through to the kitchen, barefoot and with my dressing gown cord trailing. The wine was unopened on the table, so too the Kettle Chips I'd bought. I didn't want to look at them. I ran the taps until the water was cold, splashing it in my face and filling and draining a tumbler. I watched the wind get up, a willow tree's branches snap and crack like whips and a newspaper take off. I was downing my second glass when I heard the boards groan. I crept over to the door and had a squint through the keyhole. Someone had put a crisp box on the landing and piled up some dust-sheets. I made sure I was covered up and fixed my dressing gown cord in a knot. I left the door on the latch and crossed the landing. Helen's door was ajar. I tapped it and said,

'Hello. Anyone about?' I pushed the door gently. A window had been opened and the curtains flapped about.

'Is anyone in?' I said. My nose wrinkled at the nip of bleach. A mug was upturned on the worktop. A sheath of papers was stuffed in a busted wicker basket. I bent down and picked them out, snapping off an elastic band and revealing last year's calendar. My heart sank. Where the chair and settee would've been there were dents in the carpet. A missing painting or print had left a clean patch of white emulsion on the wood chip. There were spent joss sticks and drips of candle wax on the fire surround.

'You alright, bud?'

I turned, startled. A man in paint-spattered jeans and a grubby T-shirt was wiping his hands on a rag.

'You live next door, don't you?' He smiled as if amused by something. 'Ron mentioned you.'

I nodded. I was already backing out, embarrassed at my stripy towelling dressing gown.

'Looks like you're going to have some company at last,' he said. 'It's taken forever to let this place.'

Shared
Nick Fogg

Little more than a shadow, David drags the demons of thirty-something years to the summit of the boulder-carbuncled hill. He stares at the view, not daring to breathe it in.

A skylark agitates the pale, early summer, sky. Clouds hunch along the horizon.

Barely discernible, a decision flickers across David's face. He lunges forward, summoning every ounce of energy, and races for his life towards the edge.

As his feet thrash through the grass to where the ground falls steeply away, freedom tantalisingly close, a cacophony of voices scream, 'No!' Hands grab.

David sprawls face down, spitting dust. A youth in a hoodie pins his legs. A small boy clings to his back, howling with fear.

In therapy.

David squints in the sunlight, trained on him through the consulting room window. He retreats deeper into the cushions.

'So much is blank.'

Anna nods, understanding. 'It'll take time David. You've a lot to catch up. But we can work through it together.'

She sees the dread that's wound around him tighten. The searing vividness with which the old memories surface is etched into his face.

She reaches forward, a reassuring hand on his arm. 'Have you thought any more about meeting the others? I think it'll help.'

He shakes his head, almost as if he is trying to dislodge something.

When David isn't there, someone else is.

Hunched in a corner of the police cell, dishevelled and hungover, David flinches as the viewing panel in the door clangs open. He searches the policeman's face for clues, trying to assess the damage he's done. He has no memory of how he got there.

As David waits in the interview room, familiar waves of foreboding rising, he wishes he could sink beneath them and steep himself in oblivion.

Anna smiles, reassuring, as a policeman ushers her in. She sits beside David, who braces himself.

The policeman leafs through the file, paperwork-weary. He eyes David with a mixture of fascination and disgust.

'She says she doesn't want to press charges. Nor does the club manager.'

Anna nods, relieved. David's body relaxes almost imperceptibly, but his mind is hunting desperately for the memory of who 'She' is, and what he did this time.

The policeman addresses Anna confidentially. 'What's wrong with him? Last night he was raging and swearing, this morning he's sucking his thumb.'

Shame crawls over David. He is a freak show.

And then there are the old memories.

Light from a silent TV flickers across the room, strobing glimpses of a teenage bolt-hole. Something clatters over downstairs with a muffled curse. The TV snaps off.

A shadow retreats into the darkness as footsteps pad up the

stairs a little unsteadily. They pause on the landing.

'Mummy's coming to find you.'

In the gap behind the open door, fourteen-year-old Sean huddles deeper into his hoodie. He takes a long swig of something that promises to quell the coursing adrenaline, and numb reality.

He gags as Mother's heady perfume wafts into the room. Silhouetted in the doorway, she undoes her dress and lets it slip to the floor. There is nowhere to go. No oblivion at the bottom of the bottle.

Mother steps out of her dress and across the threshold.

In group therapy.

A circle of plastic chairs seems to crowd the room. The group is almost entirely male, David the oldest. Some are attentive, others seemingly lost in their own thoughts.

Anna begins. 'I'd like to talk about what happened in the nightclub.'

David shakes his head in frustration: his memory is still blank.

Across from him, twenty-year-old Tom shifts uncomfortably, dreading the questioning turning to him. Both his arms are raked and hatched with scars. Blood seeps through a fresh dressing.

Five-year-old Jack sprawls on the floor drawing. Dark coloured crayons. His small threadbare teddy lolls beside him, watching.

Anna is gently persistent. 'Sean can you tell me about it?'

Now in his mid-twenties, Sean leans tauntingly on the back of David's chair, tipping it. David has completely withdrawn, shut down.

'Yeah.' Sean is struggling, even with the bare minimum. 'I saw her, dancing. She was looking at me.' His voice tightens. He laughs, trying to break the tension. 'I was like, 'Don't touch me, you filthy whore!' And then...' He flexes his fist at Anna trying to provoke a reaction.

Completely unmoved, she nods. 'Did you find her attractive?'

Sean's discomfort bristles. He tries to shrug it off.

'How did she make you feel Sean?'

He stares at Anna confused, horrified. She is probing a raggedly-raw nerve. He pulls a small bottle from his pocket and drinks heavily.

'Fuck her!'

Again Anna nods, inviting him to elaborate. But Sean is a long way from being able to acknowledge, let alone articulate, his feelings.

'Bitch!' He returns to his chair, slumping into it, hoodie up. Silence.

There must be a way out.

Darkness. Something soft and heavy thuds down wooden stairs. A key turns. A sickly-yellow light glows on, ineffectively lighting an old brick cellar. A hand fumbles for a wedge and shoves it under the door.

An old sweat-soaked, urine-stained mattress is dragged into the pool of light created by the simple light shade.

A torch methodically probes the shadows. The cellar is bare, solidly constructed, the corners draped with dust-clogged cobwebs.

A toe knocks out the wedge and the feet leave. The door closes quickly and heavily, the light still on. There is no longer a handle on the inside: no way of opening the door.

In therapy again.

The others occupy the same plastic chairs. David has withdrawn into his.

Sophie paces, caged within the circle. Her vibrant red lip-gloss seems too brash for her delicate mid-twenties complexion.

'My mother liked it when it was just the two of us. We'd share make-up, sometimes.'

Sean's snort of disgust rips open cracks in the memory. Some of the others mutter disapproval.

Sophie begins to wither. 'I hate being the only girl. They don't understand.' Anna nods, sympathetic.

'Now no one wants me. They think I'm a freak.' Fighting back tears, Sophie fumbles for a mirror and wipes the lip-gloss off with a tissue.

'What your mother did was very wrong. But talking about it, all together, will help.'

Unconvinced, Sophie drags her chair away from the others.

'Sophie?' Nothing.

David looks up at Anna from his chair, dazed. Smudges of lip-gloss stain his mouth.

'Hello David.'

Some of the others are children.

Jack waits at the bus stop, his bag packed. A little boy with an escape plan.

Scuffing loose stones with the toe of his shoe, he delights in the dust that clings to the fresh polish. He squats to examine a line of ants, then pushes together a mound of earth for them to climb, careful not to bury any.

Children chatter. Jack stares out of the window of the bus, absent-mindedly licking the icing off an Iced Gem.

Two little girls peer through the gap between the seats in

front, whispering.

'Did your Mummy make your lunch?' one ventures cheekily. Her friend sniggers. A woman across the aisle hushes them.

Catapulted back, David follows the girls' gaze to the seat beside him. He glances into the bag, confused.

'Mum, this man's got a kid's bag!'

Scattering Iced Gems, David grabs the bag and stumbles, head down, towards the front of the bus. Trying to blot out the accusatory stares, and whisperings of 'Paedo', he almost throws himself out of the door as soon it stops.

David bursts into Anna's room, acutely agitated. 'I can't do this any more.' He brandishes the bag at her.

'It's okay David, sit down.' Anna opens the bag. A part-eaten jam sandwich, a toothbrush, and a small grubby teddy. He looks at her imploringly.

'I think these are Jack's. He's the youngest. He loves to draw, like you used to.'

Anna unfolds a crumpled piece of paper and hands it to David. One of Jack's pictures: a circle of open coffins, sad faces.

Despair engulfs David as he comprehends. Jack knows about his plan.

Anna puts a hand on his arm, supportive, reassuring. 'As you're reclaiming your past you're reshaping their future. It's understandable they're resistant. They're still trying to protect you.'

His face darkens. 'He's a useless, pathetic, waste of space. Why should he be in charge?'

Anna starts to move, but he grabs at her breast, his breath hot on her face.

'Let go of me Sean. We talked about it, didn't we? About you all being together, supporting each other. You agreed. Do you remember?'

He stomps out, spitting, 'Interfering cunt!' over his shoulder.

Anna looks up David's notes. She writes, 'Unscheduled visit 10th August. David's anxiety heightened. Episodes of dissociation increasing again. Fear of reintegration, especially Sean and Jack. Readdress identity issues.'

Who is in control?

The cellar door opens a little. David steps in quickly through the gap. He leans heavily on the door, pushing it shut. As the latch clunks home he exhales. Somewhere in the gloom, freedom waits. He sinks onto the mattress.

Seconds later his demeanour changes. He hurls himself at the door clawing to get out.

'You bastard! What have you done?'

There are so many memories.

A child's finger carefully smoothes on bright red lip-gloss. Sophie, just ten years old, studies its effect in the mirror by the light of a dim lamp on the cluttered dressing table. Footsteps creak along the landing.

'David?'

Knowing she's as good as caught, Sophie hurriedly replaces the lip-gloss.

'I'm here Mummy.'

The footsteps bring the clink of glass and bottle. The door pushes open and Mother leans in the doorway. She slurs, sarcastic, 'Don't you look lovely!'

Sophie looks back at her reflection, uncertain. 'I'm sorry, I…'

Mother's fingers languorously caress Sophie's shoulder. 'We're going to have such a grown-up evening. Girls together. Come and sit on Mummy's bed.'

Escape.
Curled on the filthy mattress in the cellar, David's body is racked
with sobs. 'Let me out... I want out!' A phone is ringing upstairs
in the house.

He hauls himself up and checks his pockets. Then begins
feverishly searching the mattress. A smile creeps across his face
as he discovers a penknife hidden in a hole.

A circle of coffins.
Days later, the phone is ringing again. David lies crumpled on
the floor, barely conscious. His sleeves pushed up, he bleeds
from deep, purposeful cuts to his jaggedly-scarred arms. His
blood snakes patterns across the floor, congealing in the dust.

Sean stands over him. 'You idiot! We're all gonna die.'

David doesn't respond. The phone is still ringing. Discover-
ing the penknife, Sean attacks the door.

Jack is curled on the mattress sucking his thumb. Sophie lies
beside him, stroking his hair. Others from the therapy sessions
sit in the shadows, watching, waiting, scared.

Anna puts the phone down and frowns at her diary: two missed
sessions. Someone always kept the appointments - if not David,
one of the others. Could she fit in a visit? She consults the thick
file for an address.

David is slumped on the mattress, still bleeding. Footsteps echo
above. His eyes flit, delirious. The shadows of the others fall
across the floor around him.

Anna's voice calls from upstairs. His body stiffens with fear.
He peers blearily at his arms, blood shrouding his hands. He
raises a finger to his lips. Red lip-gloss. His eyes glaze.

David reaches the summit of the hill, bloody, exhausted. He breathes in the view.

Anna's footsteps descend the cellar stairs.

Summoning the last of his energy, David launches himself towards the cliff edge. Broken, rasping, voices scream out. Hands flail weakly, but he hurtles on, evading their grasp. His feet kick into the air.

The cellar door handle turns.
  'David, it's Anna. Are you down here?'

Relief envelops David as he falls. The late-summer breeze tousles his hair. He smiles.

A Thousand Hours
Tim Jeffreys

'Do you dream about me when you sleep?' he would say to her. 'Do you dream about me like I dream about you?' Because she never answered he would sit up half the night, staring at bursts of static on a screen, imagining forms and faces like a child watching clouds on a summer's day and saying, 'There's a puppy dog, there's a witch, there's me, there's you, there's me.' But really the child knows that it's only clouds.

Just like Ryker knew, if he was being honest with himself, that on his screen there was only static.

'I didn't used to believe in it,' Ryker would tell people whenever he got the opportunity. 'But now I do because I've found it. I've found it with her. With Gen. Sure I've had feelings before, right? But not like this. Never like this. There's not the smallest doubt in my mind that what Gen and I have is true love. The kind of love you hear about in all the songs. The kind of love you never really understand until you've felt it. Something real.' People would sometimes laugh or snigger when he said this, but that didn't bother him. He wrote it off as jealousy. He knew what they were thinking. Gen was young. Gen was beautiful. How did this sad-sack fifty-six year old man end up with a woman like that? 'He must have a lot of cash in the bank, eh?

Eh? Look at his job. Nice tidy salary.'

But they were wrong. The truth was he didn't have a lot of cash in the bank. Although he worked as a rep for Amanko-Doyle, one of the world's largest pharmaceutical companies, most of the money he earned disappeared into the black hole of rent and alimony payments. Gen wasn't a gold-digger. Sure, he took her shopping sometimes for clothes, or wigs, or make-up, but he only did that because he loved to treat her. Gen never expected it of him. Never, never, never.

'Gen's my soulmate.' he would tell people. 'She's like the other half of me. I know her mind. It's like…I never realised just how lonely I was until I found her.'

He knew some people were angry and disgusted by their relationship; like his ex-wife Nadine who would groan and grit her teeth and make claws with her hands and cast her eyes wildly around as if looking for something to strangle whenever Ryker told her that he and Gen were the same age mentally. The way Ryker saw it Nadine had a right to be bitter. It couldn't have been easy finding herself replaced by a younger, prettier model. She'd been fine, of course, when his relationship with Gen had been purely sexual. She'd even encouraged it. She understood that he got lonely on those long business trips, and having sex with Gen was far preferable to his previous method of coping which involved experimenting with the samples he carried around in his suitcase. Before that he'd tried visiting bars or restaurants, tried striking up conversations with strangers, men and women, but with little success. Everyone seemed locked into their own worlds. They had their friends, what did they need him for? He had no friends at home because he was always away. And he couldn't make friends on the road because he was always a stranger. Who could blame him for dabbling in pharmaceuticals? They were right there in his bag after all. Biphetamine to get him out of bed in the morning; maybe some Tramadol to see him through the day; then Fluoxetine for the evening hours when he was stuck in some hotel room with only pay-per-view porn for entertainment and that he'd found only compounded his loneliness. He hadn't needed any of those drugs though after Gen began joining him on his trips. After a while, even when he was at home and kissed Nadine's neck and pressed his erect penis against her hip, she would bat at him with her hands and tell him, 'Where's Gen? Go work it out on Gen.' 'I love you, Nadine' he would say. 'You're my wife. Don't you know I love you?'

'Love?' she would say. 'What is love? Go love Gen.' And so he did. In truth at that point in his life the only way he got hard was by thinking about Gen. With Nadine it was a case of hiking up her nightie for five minutes of missionary position sex in the dark. In bed with Gen, the only limit was his imagination. Gen didn't care that he was not as fit as he used to be, or that he had a belly these days, or that his hairline was receding, or that he sweated a lot. Gen was always accommodating.

'The night should have a thousand hours,' Gen would say in her soft voice afterwards, as they lay gazing into each other's eyes. 'The night should have a thousand hours.'

Some nights, when he got tired of staring into all that static, he would step out onto the balcony for some air. Fifty floors below, the city lay in darkness. Rooms. Locked rooms. That was how Ryker pictured it in his mind. A million locked rooms; inside which people slept, some singly, some in couples, but all alone, alone, alone inside their locked little rooms. If he raised his eyes, on clear nights he could see the stars. He would gaze at them not in wonder but with a kind of dreadful, cowed fascination, the way one might stare into those sink-holes that had begun opening up around the city swallowing buildings and stop-signs and cars and people, not out of desire but in awe, in horror, from the sheer inability to wrench the eyes away. A hollow feeling would fill him and if he stared too long at the night sky he would begin to shiver. He would draw a blanket tight around his shoulders but this would not quell the shuddering of his body.

Nadine's sympathy and understanding had eventually come to an end one day when, after returning from a business trip, Ryker confessed that he and Gen had fallen in love.

'That's it!' Nadine had said. 'Either she goes or you both go!' Ryker had only been able to bow his head. For him, there was no longer a choice. If Gen had to go, of course he'd go with her. How could he not? He loved her. She loved him; he was certain of it. She'd never said it, out loud, but then she didn't have to. It was written in her face, in her eyes, in the way she looked at him. Clearly Nadine had done her best to influence the children, which saddened Ryker. He thought it was a low blow. Both Reece and Walter refused to acknowledge Gen. They would make fun of Gen in private when they thought their father wasn't listening, and refer to her as 'that' or 'it'. Plus whenever the four of them did anything together in public – always at Ryker's insistence – they would look sheepish and embarrassed until Ryker lost his patience and was forced to make a scene. 'Listen,' he would say to them. 'I love you guys, but we can't go on like this.'

In his imagination Ryker saw Reece and Walter tearing up and saying, 'We love you too Dad!' and they would have a group hug, Gen included, and from that moment on things would be better. But this never happened. His declaration only seemed to embarrass the boys further. Then during the car ride home he would hear them in the back seat mimicking his voice and making fun of him. 'I love you guys. Bluuurgh! Ha ha! What a tool. What a pussy.'

Ryker asked Gen what she thought about this. Did it upset her? Should he punish Reece and Walter? Should he speak to Nadine about it? Gen didn't answer. She just showed him the same calm expression she always did: head slightly tilted to one side, eyes soft, lips slightly apart as if she were about to impart some wisdom but restrained herself because the answer was right there, wasn't it? Her face told him everything he needed to know, and he nodded and said: 'You're right. You're right. They just need time.' Unlike his ex-wife, Gen wasn't much of a talker and Ryker found this soothing. They could be alone together for hours and not say a word. That was the mark of a solid relationship, surely, when you didn't feel the need to make constant chit-chat? Nadine talked even when she was eating, and he'd had to watch the food rolling around in her mouth and occasionally spilling out. Gen used words sparingly, and they were always the right words for any situation. 'The night should have a thousand hours.' That was Ryker's favourite thing Gen said. Always at night after he'd finished making love to her.

'Before,' he whispered to her one night as he held her in his arms, 'I used to wish that a sink-hole would swallow me. I know, I know, it was silly to think like that. But it's true. I used to pray for it. I used to imagine there was a sink-hole somewhere that wanted me. Like it was waiting. It was kind of a comfort, I suppose, to think that something wanted me. Even a sink-hole. 'Please, please,' I used to think to myself, 'let it be today'.' He smiled and placed his hand over hers. 'But don't worry, my love, that was the past. I don't think that way any more.' He waited a moment, but Gen said nothing. Her eyelids fluttered, she gave a sweet little sigh, closed her eyes and Ryker heard the hum of her internal systems shutting down. At this point he had to get out of bed, walk around to Gen's side, open the flap in the back of her head, take the charger from the drawer, and plug Gen into the mains. This had become a strict routine, as on the odd occasion he'd forgotten Gen wouldn't wake up the next day. Spending a day without her left him thoroughly miserable.

He didn't know exactly what he was looking for in all that static. It pained him to think Gen could go somewhere he couldn't follow. That thing she always said before sleep: 'The night should have a thousand hours.' He turned its meaning over in his mind. Once he'd thought it meant she wanted more time to lie there snuggled up next to him. It was just a cute thing she said before she closed her eyes. But now he wondered, did she in fact mean she wanted more time away from him, more time asleep, more time inside her own head, lost somewhere in that fog of static where he couldn't reach her any more? With each passing day, something gnawed at him. He became more and more convinced it was the latter.

One day when Gen was in the bath and Ryker was washing her as he loved to do - first rubbing the soap into her shoulders, then working it down her arms, then onto her breasts and belly - Gen said in her soft, lilting, sweet but vaguely hollow-sounding voice, 'Fuck you, Ryker.'

'What?' Ryker fell back on his heels. He held his bubble-covered hands before him. Tears welled in his eyes. 'Fuck you, Ryker. You're old and you're fat and you smell like stale cheese. When you touch me it makes my skin crawl.'

He stared at her with his mouth agape. She sat quite still in the waist-high water gazing back at him. Her face had its usual expression, but now it looked as if she were mocking him, waiting for his reaction. Relief washed through him when he realised what must have happened. Reece and Walter had visited the previous weekend and had spent most of it hunched over the Cloudhub giggling and whispering to each other. They must have found a way to hack into Gen's hard drive and altered some of her vocal settings. 'Those little bastards!' he said, standing.

After drying his hands, he tossed the towel aside, stormed into the lounge and turned on the Cloudhub. He then spent four hours having a series of web-chats with customer service agents at The Honeystore. At first they thought there might be a problem with what they called Gen's 'mindbox'. They explained to Ryker how to remotely link his Cloudhub to Gen's hardrive, after which he would be able to view the mindbox and see if there was a problem. 'You mean,' typed Ryker, 'that I'll be looking into her thoughts?' 'In a manner of speaking, yes.' typed the customer service agent. 'Think of it as her control centre. You'll be able to look through her eyes, and see what information she's processing about her situation. But you'll also be able to access her mindbox, where all that information's assessed.'

Ryker had suddenly felt a bolt of fear pass through him. What if he did look into her thoughts and discovered that she actually did despise him?

'Oh no,' he typed, 'it's the vocal settings, I'm sure. Can't we just get them reset to shop-bought standard?'

'No problem at all.' typed the agent, and proceeded to unfurl the instructions on how to do this. He also explained to Ryker how he could, if he wished, personalise Gen's mindbox, perhaps even implant his own fantasies and desires so that Gen would act them out for him. But Ryker said no. He wanted Gen the way she was, the way she'd always been. He didn't want to change or influence her in any way.

'Just a reminder,' the agent typed. 'The option's there if you want it.' 'Just tell me how to reset her mindbox back to how it was before,' Ryker typed. 'That's all I want.' By the time Ryker returned to the bathroom, the water Gen sat in was icy-cold although she still had that half-smile on her face. He found this disturbing, but he pushed the thought away. 'My darling, I'm so sorry!' he said as he lifted her out of the tub and got a couple of towels around her as fast as he could. 'How could I have left you alone for so long?' No one could have blamed her if she'd said 'Fuck you, Ryker!' at that moment, but she didn't. Instead, her eyes fluttered, her lips parted and she said, 'I love the way you hold me.' Hearing this, tears welled once more in Ryker's eyes and he lifted her and carried her into the bedroom. 'It was just a little glitch,' he said, as he sat Gen down on the bed and began drying her. 'Everything's back to normal now.' He looked at Gen's face. Her mouth had opened again as if she might speak. When she didn't he felt another wave of relief. The next time Reece and Walter visited, he confronted them about hacking into Gen's hard-drive and altering her vocal settings so that she'd say mean things to Ryker, but they swore they hadn't. 'Anyway,' Reece, who'd been getting lippy since he turned thirteen, said, 'Gen has a mind of her own. Doesn't she?'

Once, only once, the static broke and for a few seconds he saw something else appear on the screen. At first he thought that it might be his own face, appearing right there before his eyes as though from a fog. But then the screen flickered, the image sharpened, Ryker drew closer to the screen, and he saw that it was a sink-hole. A great, deep, circular sink-hole; the same one that had been on the news the previous day, the one that had

swallowed an entire school on the other side of the city, swallowed it children and all. He could remember thinking: How deep does that thing go? He had imagined lying in the dark at the bottom of the hole, lying there all alone. If anyone survived falling into that thing, how long would they lie there waiting for someone to rescue them? A hundred hours? A thousand…? Ryker blinked, shuddered, and the image was gone.
After that he saw only the formless static.

Through My Own Fault
Tim Franks

Pausing, only in his mind, to squeeze Sister Mary Bartholomew to his chest and whisper, 'Who luvs ya baby?' Father Michael Devine made his way to the confessional. Equipped with his stole, breviary, vacuum flask, and digestive biscuits he was ready for business. He hated doing confessions at the convent. As a silent, enclosed order the list of possible sins was distinctly limited. But as this was one of the few opportunities the good ladies had to converse, it was inevitable that they should indulge in a little embellishment to preserve the interview. With precise feet, he eased his way up the aisle. In his own church, his movements were swift and breezy. Familiarity with the Supreme Being made him nonchalant in His presence, but the sisters had certain standards. They demanded every movement was coloured by a professional solemnity, so he was their black chameleon. Like a jury, the bent black queue knelt, ready to imprison him. Before facing them, he genuflected to a small altar, crossed himself, and turned. Then they were before him. Each wimpled brow leaned floor-wards, eyes watching fingers, rosaries rotating. Still, Father Devine had no interest in the faces; he felt personal involvement should be avoided in sacramental matters.

Under sentence of deathly boredom, he was sealed into his coffin of a confessional. Good Friday; he shouldn't be here. He'd heard their confessions on Wednesday, and with a full week's sinning behind them the nuns' offences weren't worth the breath he used absolving them. Today would be an interminable monotony of invention, as the nuns searched their sterile lives for a bacterium of sin and found themselves guilty only of being guiltless. Father Devine despised Holy Week. It was all so pointless. This wasn't the reason he'd become a priest. In the seminary, he'd always been recognised as an outstanding student. He'd revelled in the intellectual crossfire of theology, using Saint John or Tom Paine with equal delight to splinter his friends upon the rack of ethical morality.

His mind filled the dark box with memories of St Dominic's, his first parish. He'd been sent as an assistant to Father Thornley, and had felt satisfied there. Many evenings he'd sat in the presbytery and destroyed the old man's simple philosophies; debasing his observations of life with Greek and Latin quotations. Those were good days. It had been a real parish, a city parish. Now he sat waiting for the first empty doll to come in and begin her mechanical dialogue. He'd wanted so much more; expected it. He'd gained a distinction in sociology.

Then the door opened. A shuffling of garments was followed by a soft voice. 'Bless me Father for I have sinned. It has been forty-eight hours since my last confession…'

As the sister magnified peccadilloes, Father Devine's mind wandered on a secular romance of axe murders, narcotics, bodies in bridge foundations, lace-clad girls with stilettos tucked in their suspenders, and various bodily appendages distributed via the Royal Mail.

'That's all, Father.' The nun apologised and lapsed into silence. Father Devine paused. He always made them wait upon his judgement. The excitement did them good. 'Go out and whip your naked body with a barbed thong, then rub salt and cinders into the wounds with a horsehair glove. And may God have mercy on your leprous soul,' he thought. But his mouth said 'Two Hail Marys sister, and say a prayer for me.'

Sister followed sister, each the same as the last. Sin upon sin was breathed onto the grill, but none penetrated to touch the priest. Steadfastly, he ignored all opportunities to talk. Often he was elsewhere, as his mind amused itself trying to invent the ultimate penance. Still the time dragged out hatefully. Two and a half hours of trivia eked by. The flask was empty and the digestive biscuits were reduced to a pile of crumbs in the lap of his cassock. He had hardly heard a sin he'd pardoned. Blankly he stared, forgetting where he was and thinking of last night. On Thursday evenings he dressed in jeans and a tee-shirt, and went for a drink with the lads. The lads were the young priests who worked locally, most had been at his seminary. Each week they met in the same upstairs bar, around the same table, drinking beer and swapping stories. Last night they'd all been late after making their annual act of humility: washing feet. At least the bunions and grimy toenails had given Father Devine a platform. Weaving stories from talcum powder and foot odour, using grains of truth he'd built an illusion, like a conjuror. He'd felt good with all the eyes upon him. This was what he excelled at, what it had always been like, before he was re-assigned; before he'd begun to sit toward the end of the table and men like Colm had eased towards the centre.

Father Devine had always been an admired raconteur, but now he found himself more and more a listener while others took his role. Oh, Colm was interesting, amusing even, but he just told bare facts. He lacked Father Devine's power of seizing upon tragedy and human weakness and distilling them into entertainment. Given half a story Colm was no match for him. But his work was just too much of a handicap. He was a lonely wanderer in a desert of veniality. Over the months he had felt his purpose in life being eroded. How could he enthral an audience with stories of a nun's jealousy about another sister's skill at embroidery?

Isolation fuelled his mind with nostalgia, and it travelled back to Saint Dominic's: plenty of life there, and he'd watched all go by with a rare interest. What a mix of people crawled along those streets. Sandwiched between slum clearance and the dock gates, Saint Dominic's had provided a show he'd never guessed existed. His world had been neat, with trees, and God, and Mass. Aged twelve he was deemed to have heard the Lord's voice and entered the seminary, where, distanced from distractions, he was taught about theology, and Mass, and life. Then he had been in the thick of it, humanity and violence, intrigue and sin; while the privilege of his black shirt and white collar allowed him to walk all over this scurrying colony untouched, unless he chose to pet a child. He'd felt like a real priest then. So much to talk about. He was never ignored. Not like today.

Where were the men like Mahon now? How he'd had the lads crying with laughter at the tales of the tiny figure cycling between his wife and two mistresses, all in various stages of pregnancy. What a picture he'd painted of this bantam of a man on his bicycle, wispy red hair trailing behind him, and never sitting on the saddle, due to the tenderness of his equipment. He'd excelled himself with that yarn, especially when he'd embarked upon the old parish priest's imaginary monologue with himself, torn between admonishing Mahon for his infidelity, and praising him for so strictly following papal pronouncements on contraception and maintaining a Catholic population in an increasingly pagan world. Boredom had been a stranger to him then. Thursdays had been great. As he speculated on the brevity of his stay at Saint Dominic's, he was oblivious to the parallelogram of light clicking shut yet again. Another shadowy figure knelt behind the purple curtain, its head quartered by a crucifix. Father Devine uttered a heartfelt prayer. 'Are there many waiting Sister?'

'No Father, I'm the last. Another monotone mumbled the magic formula, and the priest awaited more selections from the convent's small catalogue of offences. 'In a premeditated way Father, I have abused a sacrament. One of my sins is lying in confession.'

Surprised into attention Father Devine leaned towards the grill. 'For many months now I have said, 'That's all Father', but it has not been all. In fact it's been almost nothing. The truth is that I have been regularly enjoying a passionate and deeply carnal affair with a muscular young man, who came last Spring to repaint the outside of the chapel. The first touch was accidental - at least on my part. I was strolling in the small flower garden. It was a lovely day and I wanted to feel alive before I faced my silent sisters at lunch. I remember thinking it would be grand if I could just sit down, hitch up my skirts and roll down my thick black stockings to feel the sun's warm fingers on my legs, like I used to as a girl. No one was watching, so I sat on the grass anyway. I thought I was alone, until I saw his figure sprawled beneath a ladder. He's fallen, I thought and felt inadequate. I was afraid of his injuries... and his shorts. Slowly, I crept over and knelt before his almost naked body, and touched his cheek to see if he was conscious. He was sunbathing, and when his smiling eyes opened, and he joked about my soft hands...' Her voice dissolved upon the memory. Father Devine's mouth moved, but his mind was unable to give it words. None of the stock phrases applied and reality smothered his imagination. Avidly he stared at the silhouette, waiting. His only desire was to know what happened next. Sensing the shock she had created, the nun spoke into the silence. 'In the privacy of the tool store, at the far end of the vegetable plot, we experienced each other regularly and totally for a number of months. Do you know Father, for years I'd lain in my dark cell knowing no one else's touch but my own, dreaming of a man's hand's, trying to imagine the sensation, and here he was, hands and more. An answer to a prayer you might say.' Once more her tale was interrupted and, after a pause, Father Devine heard a sound which he took to be muffled weeping. Calling up every fibre of his professionalism he felt compelled to be magnanimous. 'It...' his voice cracked, so he started again. 'It is a blessing that you have come here to ask God's forgiveness.' His words fell like bricks. Shuffling solid seminary platitudes, he was unable to arrange a wall of self-protection. 'Think of the parable of the lost sheep, Sister. That will give you... reassurance. It is a credit to your faith that... that you have... laid aside this man, and... to your self control.' 'Self-control, my arse, Father. Laid aside this man? He's gone, or I'd be laid under him, not here. Two weeks ago he came to me, as usual, and afterwards, quite conversationally, mentioned that he was moving into a flat with his girlfriend and this was to be his last visit. In confusion I wept that I needed him, but as I gripped him, sobbing, his next remark drove out every emotion except one. He said he'd arrange, for one of his friends to come instead of him, so that would be all right. 'Keep your frustration at bay,' he said. 'Keep you relaxed.' Then he lay back on a pile of sacks and closed his eyes. I just stared at him until I heard his smug snores. Then I used a mallet to hammer the screwdriver into his ear. He didn't bleed much, and it was never really his mind I was interested in. It was dark outside and no one would come down from the convent at that time of night so I set to work. For three hours I sweated to dig a hole deeper than the gardeners ever go. The soil is always being freshly turned over there, so by the time I'd spread out the earth his body had replaced you couldn't notice a thing. I think that's all Father... Unless you need to hear about me entertaining a little resentment against Sister...' 'No, no. That won't be necessary,' the priest stammered. Then,clinging to his office like a straw, he said, 'Now make a good act of contrition for your sins.' His lips mumbled unconscious words as his mind tried to absorb what he had just heard. It was an uneven struggle and, unaware that he had finished speaking, he was suspended in silence. 'Father, my penance,' reminded the nun, in quiet voice.

'For your penance say... say... say... Three Hail Marys, and say a prayer for me, Sister.'

Instead of slinking away with a respectful 'Thank you Father,' the nun spoke again.

'Do you know Father I don't think I'll be saying that penance at all. I don't give a damn about your absolution. I just wanted to see what punishment your finely trained mind felt to be compatible with my sins. The finest fruits of two thousand years of human experience and divine guidance: three Hail Marys. Still Father maybe you shouldn't punish me. After all I haven't really killed him. I've worked a miracle. The miracle of the resurrection. Next Spring I'll make him rise again, and we'll all be able to receive him, body and blood, as his flesh rots to nourish the cabbages. Then he'll live again in the sisters. Tell me, Father, does church law classify letting a man enter your body in the form of a cabbage as a technical loss of virginity?' Again there was silence, but the nun made no offer to break Father Devine's unease.

Eventually his timid voice staggered, 'When will you be

leaving the convent Sister?'

'Leaving? Oh, I won't be leaving, Father. No, I couldn't leave my man behind. I must be faithful.'

'But...'

'Why shouldn't I stay? I think I'm well suited to the work. Granted I won't raise my heart to God, but my head will bow and my lips move at all the right times, and really isn't that all that's required?'

'Three Hail Marys, Father,' she derided. 'I'm not sure who has the least imagination - you for that penance, or God for thinking you'd make a priest.'

The door opened, and light briefly invaded the box, before darkness reclaimed the space.

Father Devine's mind gasped like an athlete forced beyond the limits of his inadequate training. Hours evaporated as he tried to tear answers from his personal experiences and Greek and Latin quotations. But he'd never used them compassionately for others and they were useless to him now. So he sat, adrift in the dark, untouched by time. It was the chapel bell that jolted him back into reality. And when, finally, he emerged, the nuns were gathered for their Good Friday liturgy, ready to mourn the death of their saviour. In the face of his revealed self, he retreated behind the shield of his priesthood. Then he genuflected and prepared, once again, to ply his trade beneath the red light. As he walked towards the altar, his eyes searched the anonymous rows. Not an eye glimmered, nor a cheek reddened; and he knew that he would never know. And worse, that he could never tell.

The Writers

ANNA SALONEN has been exploring imaginary worlds ever since she could pick up a book, and she loves speculative fiction in all its forms. Her short stories have been published in Finnish and in English. Apart from writing, her other interests include classic literature, mythology, and Victoriana. When she's not writing she enjoys museum visits, console games, and playing superhero ninja pirates with her niece and nephew. She lives in Turku, Finland with her husband.

JILL HAND is a former newspaper reporter and editor from New Jersey. She is a member of the Horror Writers Association. Her work has appeared in more than thirty publications and in eight anthologies. Her time travel novella, *The Blue Horse*, featuring George Booth-Grey, the eccentric seventh Earl of Stamford and his one-of-a kind steed, won a winter 2017 Pinnacle Achievement Award for best fantasy book from the National Association of Book Entrepreneurs.

VALENTINE WILLIAMS lives in an untidy cottage in Shropshire with her first and only husband and their fourth son. She has published a number of dark fiction novels, poetry, and commissioned non-fiction works. She started a writers' group in her home town which is still going strong, and her poetry has won several major prizes. Mantle Lane Press recently published her short story collection, *A Far Cry*.

KAREN BOVENMYER earned an MFA in Creative Writing: Popular Fiction from the University of Southern Maine. She teaches and mentors students at Iowa State University. She is the 2016 recipient of the Horror Writers Association Mary Wollstonecraft Shelley Scholarship. Her poems, short stories and novellas appear in more than forty publications and her first novel, *Swift for the Sun*, an LGBT romantic adventure in 1820s Caribbean, debuted from Dreamspinner Press in March 2017.

M. REGAN has been writing in various capacities for over a decade, with credits ranging from localization work to scholarly reviews, advice columns to poetry. Particularly fascinated by those fears and maladies personified by monsters, she enjoys composing dark fiction and studying supernatural creatures.

LISA DE YOUNG lives in a small town in Northwest Indiana, with her husband and three daughters, where she manages a dental office. She enjoys writing fiction in her spare time and is a member of the Horror Writers Association. Her short stories and poetry have appeared in over 10 publications including Deadman's Tome Book of Horrors II, The Voices Project and Trigger Warning.

SIMON KEWIN is the author of over one hundred published short stories. His works have appeared in Nature, Daily Science Fiction, Abyss & Apex and many more. He lives in England with his wife and their daughters. His cyberpunk novel The Genehunter and his Cloven Land fantasy trilogy were recently published.

PETRA KUPPERS is a disability culture activist, a community performance artist and a professor. Her most recent poetry collection is *PearlStitch* (Spuyten Duyvil: 2016). Stories have appeared in Drunken Boat, PodCastle, The Sycamore Review, Visionary Tongue, Future Fire, Accessing the Future: A Disability-Themed Anthology of Speculative Fiction, and elsewhere. She is the Artistic Director of The Olimpias, an international disability culture collective, and lives with her partner Stephanie Heit in Ypsilanti, Michigan.

JENNIFER MCLEAN is a writer and teacher who grew up in Yorkshire and now lives in Warwickshire. She has published poems, runs workshops for young writers, and was selected for Writing West Midlands' Room 204 programme. Jennifer is currently working on a novel and a poetry collection about the north. *Welcome* is her first published short story.

JOSHUA JONES' fiction has appeared in Necessary Fiction, The Tishman Review, Juked, The Golden Key, and elsewhere. He lives near Washington, D.C.

PASCALE PRESUMEY grew up in a tiny village near Lyon, in France but now lives in Burton on Trent. In 2015 she was accepted onto Writing West Midlands' writers development scheme, Room 204. Pascale's short stories have been published in magazines and anthologies both in the UK and North America and she has recently completed her novel *The Journeyman*. She is at present writing a radio script entitled *The Value of My Hair*.

GRACE HADDON writes fantasy short stories. She is a regular writer for the Big Care Write-Up, a Leicester charity initiative, and was on the judging panel for the Leicester Writes Short Story Prize. She recently completed a Creative Writing BA at the University of Nottingham, where she edited the class anthology *Vices and Virtues*. When she isn't writing, she enjoys killing zombies (in video games), collecting carnivorous plants and obsessing over Doctor Who.

ALEX SHVARTSMAN is a writer, translator and game designer from Brooklyn, NY. Over ninety of his short stories have appeared in Nature, Galaxy's Edge, InterGalactic Medicine Show, and many other magazines and anthologies. He won the 2014 WSFA Small Press Award for Short Fiction and was a two-time finalist for the Canopus Award for Excellence in Interstellar Fiction (2015 and 2017). He is the editor of the Unidentified Funny Objects annual anthology series of humorous SF/F. *Masquerade Night* was originally published in the anthology *In a Cat's Eye*, from Pole to Pole Publishing.

Irish writer TRACY FAHEY writes quiet, psychological horror. Her short fiction collection, *The Unheimlich Manoeuvre*, was published in 2016 and her short stories have appeared in fourteen US and UK anthologies. In 2016 two of her stories were long listed by Ellen Datlow for The Best Horror of the Year Volume 8. Her first novel, *The Girl In The Fort* will be published in 2017 and her second collection *New Music For Old Rituals* will appear in 2018.

SIOBHAN LOGAN'S poetry and prose collections *Firebridge to Skyshore* and *Mad, Hopeless and Possible* were published by Original Plus and performed at Ledbury Poetry Festival, the British Science Museum and National Space Centre. Her short fiction appears in various anthologies and her story *Bodywrapped* was choreographed by Belgian dance company Retina. A hypertext narrative Philae's Book of Hours was published by the European Space Agency in 2016. She teaches Creative Writing at De Montfort University.

LEE GLENWRIGHT insists that he is a far nicer person than his imagination would imply. Citing his influences as ranging from Ray Bradbury to David Cronenberg and everyone in between, his writing can also be seen in the anthology *Forever Hungry*, from Far Horizons Press, and the forthcoming *The 4th Spectral Book of Horror Stories*.
He comes from Sunderland, UK, where he lives with his family, far too many reptiles, and a dark sense of humour.

DOUGLAS FORD lives and works on the west coast of Florida, just off an exit made famous by a Jack Ketchum short story. His weird, dark fiction has appeared in Dark Moon Digest, Great Jones Street, and other publications. He and his wife share their home with several reptiles who regard them with great suspicion. He invites readers to seek him out on Facebook.

RICHARD LAKIN is a keen writer of short stories and his work has been published in the Guardian, Daily Telegraph and Structo magazine among others. He is currently completing his first novel *Garage Flowers*. He lives in Staffordshire.

NICK FOGG lives in the wilds of South Shropshire. She's a screenwriter and filmmaker, with short films screened at international film festivals and broadcast on TV. She's currently working on her first feature film projects. Nick has been selected for the London Screenwriters' Festival Talent Campus and the BFI Net.Work Midlands Talent Modules. She's also been shortlisted for the BAFTA Rocliffe New Writing Forum.
Shared is her first short story.

TIM JEFFREYS writes horror, science fiction and weird fiction - sometimes all at once. His sci-fi novella, *Voids*, co-written with Martin Greaves was published by Omnium Gatherum in 2016. His short fiction has appeared in various international anthologies and magazines. He also edits and compiles the Dark Lane Anthologies. Tim also holds an honours degree in Graphic Arts and Design. Originally from Manchester, Tim now lives in Bristol with his partner and two young daughters.

TIM FRANKS lives in Wolverhampton and has had a career in primary schools. He wrote textbooks for OUP and Pearson about history, how to write for different early reading levels, and related poems and prose. As well as short stories, he is working on his second political crime fiction novel. He is grateful for the support and encouragement he has received from Writing West Midlands and the Room 204 project.

Links

Karen Bovenmyer	www.karenbovenmyer.com
Tracy Fahey	www.designingtracy.wixsite.com/tracyfahey
Nick Fogg	www.nick-fogg.co.uk
Tim Franks	www.timfranks.org
Lee Glenwright	www.thedarkestcorneroftheroom.blogspot.com
Grace Haddon	www.gracehaddon.com
Tim Jeffreys	www.timjeffreys.blogspot.co.uk
Simon Kewin	www.simonkewin.co.uk
Petra Kuppers	www.petrakuppersfiction.wordpress.com
Richard Lakin	www.richlakin.wordpress.com
Siobhan Logan	www.siobhanlogan.blogspot.co.uk
M. Regan	www.facebook.com/mreganfiction
Anna Salonen	www.strangeandcuriousthings.blogspot.co.uk
Alex Shvartsman	www.alexshvartsman.com
Valentine Williams	www.valentinewilliams.co.uk
Jessamy Hawke	www.jessamyhawke.co.uk
Mantle Lane Press	www.mantlelanepress.co.uk

Acknowledgements

This publication was supported using public funding by the National Lottery through Arts Council England

Mantle Lane Press would like to acknowledge help and support from Writing East Midlands and Writing West Midlands.

Mantle Lane Press is a subsidiary of Mantle Arts Limited, which receives financial support from North West Leicestershire District Council.

www.ingramcontent.com/pod-product-compliance
Lightning Source LLC
Chambersburg PA
CBHW061036120726
47910CB00006B/2272